The

Mechanic

&

The MD

By Linda Shenton

Matchett

The Mechanic and the MD

By Linda Shenton Matchett

Cover Design and author photo by: Wes Matchett

PHOTO CREDITS: Woman in Jeep: iStock by Getty Images/SDI Productions, Doctor's bag: Shutterstock/Photology1971

ISBN-13: 978-1-7347085-2-3

Published by Shortwave Press

This is a work of fiction. Names, characters, places, and incidents either are the products of the author's imagination or are used fictitiously. Any resemblance to actual events or persons, living or dead, is entirely coincidental.

New Hampshire, June 1943

Chapter One

The factory's end-of-shift signal shrieked, piercing Doris Strealer's ears. She laid down the bucking bar then yanked off her red-and-white bandanna and finger-combed her brown hair. The only sister in the family with mousy brunette hair. Not russet-auburn like Emily's or corn-silk blonde like Cora's. She frowned. What did the color of her hair matter? It wasn't as if she was ever getting married. She had yet to meet a guy willing to date a tall gal, and at five foot eleven, she'd towered over every boy in high school and college. The workplace was proving no different.

Striding between the endless row of airplane wings, she walked to the time-clock station and slid her card into the machine's slot. The clock punched her card with a bang, and she returned it to its niche. She rotated her neck to ease the kinks in her shoulders. Gripping the metal bar for twelve hours a day while her partner Teresa attached thousands of rivets to airplane wings knotted her muscles like one of Grandma's homemade pretzels.

She stuffed the kerchief into her pocket and trudged to the women's locker room. Being one of America's Rosie the Riveters was nowhere near as glamorous as the magazine articles touted, but at least she wasn't stuck at a desk. She'd do almost any job to avoid holding a sedentary position.

"Want to go to the movies tonight, Doris?" Petite and pretty, Teresa had already exchanged her coveralls for a cute yellow polka-dot dress and white peep-toe shoes. "A bunch of us are going to meet up at the Majestic. The new Betty Grable musical *Coney Island* is playing. I'm sick to death of war movies, aren't you?"

"Maybe another time. It's my grandma's birthday today, and we're having a party for her."

"That sounds like fun."

Doris changed into her street clothes. "It's something to do. But the festivities won't be the same without Emily, who is overseas, and Cora is still mourning Brian's death even though it's been two years since he was killed during the Pearl Harbor attack. Not a very joyous atmosphere, but we give it a go."

"Yvonne says the war will be over by Christmas, then life can get back to normal."

"Even with the German army surrendering in Stalingrad in February and last month's victory in Tunisia, I don't think that's going to happen. The Allies have a long fight on their hands before Hitler gives up."

Teresa combed her raven-colored tresses. "Stalingrad. Tunisia. El Alamein. So many places I'd never heard of before this war started."

Doris cocked her head. "A lot has changed in the last eighteen months. Do you like your job, Teresa?"

"Well enough, I guess. Why? Don't you?"

"Not really. I'm proud to be doing something for the war effort, but I'm bored. Our work doesn't exactly require a lot of thought."

"Are you going to look for something else?" Teresa grabbed her pocketbook from inside the locker and slammed the door. She slipped her arm through the handbag's strap and headed toward the exit. "What else could you do?"

"I'd rather tinker with engines." Doris walked beside her partner. "Unfortunately, none of the garages in town will hire a female mechanic, and when I brought that issue up during my interview for this place, Mr. Meyer rolled his eyes. There must be somewhere I can work on cars or trucks."

They followed the crowd of women out of the building and walked across the street to the bus stop. Doris shielded her eyes from the pink-and-orange rays of the setting sun. "It's been over twenty years since women got the right to vote. Why don't we have the right to get the job that we want? It's not fair."

"No matter what job you secure, you're going to have to give it up when the men come home. Do you want to take a position you might love, only to lose it when the war is over?"

The six-fifteen bus shimmied and bucked as it rumbled toward them. Acrid diesel exhaust belched from the vehicle. Brakes squealed, and the lumbering beast came to a stop. Teresa coughed and waved her hand to dispel the fumes. "I like you, Doris, but I don't understand why you want to work on stinky engines." She climbed the stairs into the bus and deposited her coin in the box.

Doris followed her on board. "You may think it smells bad, but to me it's better than the scent of Evening in Paris." She sighed and dropped into the first vacant pair of seats. "Boyle Brothers and Mighty Mechanics are both hiring, but they're not accepting female applicants. They're going to be in a bind when the rest of the men are called up."

"Then you can swoop in to the rescue." Teresa grinned and sat next to her then leaned over and pointed out the window at a poster on the side of the bus stop shelter. "Or you can contact the Red Cross Motor Corps. They're looking for volunteers."

⸻

Ron McCann bent over the patient lying on the operating table and began to remove the blood-encrusted bandage on the young soldier's leg. Thunder boomed and rain pounded the windows. The lights flickered but remained illuminated. For the time being. Deplorable conditions for an operating theater.

Sweat trickled down his spine despite the chill in the massive ballroom that once held dancing couples. One of thousands of centuries-old castles requisitioned by the British, Heritage Hall now served as a convalescent hospital. After a bombing in the north end of London by the

Jerries, Heritage also acted as an overflow surgical center, today being the third time this week. He glanced across the mahogany-paneled expanse at the sea of wounded-filled gurneys. How many more young men waited in the corridors?

Piece by piece, he removed shrapnel from the boy's knees and shins then stitched the openings. Fortunately for the lad, the metal fragments had not done extensive damage. He might limp a bit but wouldn't lose either limb. On the downside, with such minor repairs required, the youngster would probably be back in combat within a matter of weeks.

Hours passed, and Ron continued to patch up American and British soldiers returning to merry old England from the lines. Most of his buddies from med school were assigned to various fronts, and he'd asked to serve nearer to the fighting, but the powers that be felt his skills were better used on English soil.

His eyes burned with fatigue, and his back screamed from hunching over the broken bodies of the boys who should be chasing girls in high school or pursuing their future in college. He was an old man in comparison. Fresh out of residency, he'd received his draft notice three months ago. A few weeks of army training, then a troop transport across the ocean, and a bumpy ride from Portsmouth to the crowded streets of Hemel Hempstead.

"This is the last patient, Dr. McCann." Sister Greene dabbed the perspiration from his forehead with a linen square clasped in a surgical clamp. He had no idea of the woman's age, but rumor had it she'd seen action during the Indian wars, the Mexican Revolution, and the Great War. Now in the twilight of her life, she was in the midst of armed conflict again. Her steely gaze and sharp tongue had sent more than a few junior cadet nurses crying into their pillows. Personality aside, she was a godsend in the operating room. Nothing caused her to flinch or faint.

"Thank you, Nurse. Another fine job. I appreciate your help." Ron snipped the last thread. He covered his work with a bandage and stepped back from the table. Two orderlies moved the patient to a gurney and wheeled him out the door to the dormitory-style ward.

"You should get some rest, Doctor."

"As should you." He smiled at the indefatigable woman. "But I'm guessing you plan something else for the remainder of the daylight hours."

A shrug lifted her shoulders. "There's inventory to be done, laundry that never ends, and as good as my staff is, I check their work to ensure the boys are getting the best possible care."

"Your work ethic and energy put me to shame, Sister Greene."

Pink tinged her cheeks, and she pressed her lips together. "Flattery will get you nowhere, Doctor."

He threw back his head and laughed, the sound echoing against the hard surfaces of the cavernous space. "Let me help you with inventory. Surgery always leaves me keyed up, so sleep is out of the question for the time being. I'd like to be of some use."

She studied him for a moment, then nodded. "Very well. I'll meet you in the dispensary. We'll begin there."

"Yes, ma'am." He touched his fingers to the side of his head in mock salute.

"You're not too old or too big for a paddling." She shook her index finger at him, but the twinkle in her eye belied her firm voice. "Ten minutes. Don't be late." She toddled through the door.

Ron removed his gloves, tossing them into an enamel bowl on the tray near the operating table, then untied the string the held the sterile gown over his uniform, dropping the soiled garment into the mesh bag propped against the wall. He walked to the sink and washed his hands, watching the orderlies and nurses clean the room and put it to rights for the next round of wounded.

He left the noise behind and hurried down the wide, gleaming staircase, its balusters individual works of art. The home's former ancestors glared at him from intricate, gilt frames, and he lifted a hand in greeting as he trotted past.

Sister Greene stood in front of a glass cabinet, holding a clipboard and wearing a deep frown.

"What is it?" He peered into the cabinet, and his eyes narrowed. The stock of pharmaceuticals, bandages, tape, and other consumables was minimal. "Did we use that much with this last influx of patients, or did the delivery fail to arrive again?"

"The latter, I'm afraid."

He raked his fingers through his hair and blew out a loud breath. "What is wrong with the army's system? We put in requisitions, and they fill them. How hard can that be?"

She opened her mouth to respond, but he held up a hand. "Strictly a rhetorical question, Nurse. I don't expect you to know the answer. Let's pray for a miracle and hope God sees fit to grant one."

Engines thrummed outside.

"If I'm not mistaken, more *visitors* just arrived." Ron frowned. "Inventory will have to wait."

"We'll be ready for you, Doctor."

"I'd expect nothing less, Sister." He flung the words over his shoulder as he raced from the room and headed to the foyer.

He pushed open the heavy front door. Outside, the raging maelstrom now simmered with a light mist and occasional thunder. A pair of ambulances parked on the gravel in front of the stone entrance. Each of the drivers held one end of a stretcher, and a hospital orderly gripped the other. They carted their loads inside. He pointed toward the ballroom, and they swept past him.

The lingering fragrance of flowers filled his nose, and he whipped his head toward the uniformed figures. Both women. With their hair stuffed underneath their tin hats, he hadn't noticed their gender. More and more of the drivers were female. What was Roosevelt thinking when he signed the order letting women into the armed forces?

Neville Thorson, a brilliant surgeon from London nudged his arm. "Your opinion is all over your face, and it's going to get you in trouble one of these days. Face it, Doctor. The gals are here to stay."

Ron shook his head. "They're to be protected and provided for, not assigned to war zones."

"Since when is England a combat zone?" Neville shoved his hands into his pockets.

"Hitler may not be bombing as regularly as he did in forty-one, but death remains a dangerous possibility every day."

"Get used to it, chap. Working side by side with the ladies is our reality." He grinned. "One for which I'm eternally grateful. Some of the drivers are real lookers."

"Women have no right in the Medical Corps, and I'm going to contact HQ about it. I don't want these women coming to my hospital."

Chapter Two

Doris stepped out of the sedan behind the other two girls who'd been assigned to Heritage Hall. A frigid wind lifted her wool cover from her head, and hurled the brimmed cap into the stone fountain in the circular driveway. She scurried to the empty basin and snatched the hat. The calendar might say August, but the weather shrieked November. She was to divide her time between the hospital and the dispatch facility in the next village. Hopefully, there would be at least a few warm days before winter set in.

She stifled a yawn as she traversed the gravel trying not to get her heel stuck in the stones. Would she be able to catch some shut-eye before jumping into her new role? Not that she could sleep with the excitement of finally being in England. The flight across the ocean in a troop transport had been exhausting and exhilarating. Being one of only two gals on an airplane full soldiers provided hours of entertainment while the men each tried to outdo the others with stories of bravery and readiness to take on the enemy. How many would still be alive at the end of the month?

Where had that maudlin thought come from? She shook her head. Squashed between the two nurses in the back of the car, she could see out the windshield as the driver navigated the crowded streets of London then the skinny, washboard roads of the countryside. She lost count of the number of times she closed her eyes when a vehicle passed them on the right side. Which would always be the wrong side as far as she was concerned.

"You okay, luv?" Amanda O'Reilly, a first generation Irish gal from Brooklyn, New York beckoned. Her flaming hair glinted in the sun, and a smile lit up her porcelain face. "Yer standing there a bit dumbfounded. Never seen a castle, have you?"

"No, and neither have you, I'd guess."

"I've seen pictures from the old country. I can't imagine havin' to heat the place, can you? My granny worked as a scullery maid at some grand estate when she was young, and she would tell us stories about how drafty and cold these monstrosities are. Worse than a barn."

"Now, you'll be able to tell your own tales of woe." Doris giggled. "And I'll be working in the barn. Maybe. Or wherever they store the trucks and ambulances."

Amanda snorted a laugh. "Oh, honey. You've got that all wrong. The people who gave up these homes have scads of money, and they've got a building for just about everything. No need for them to pile their stuff all in one place, like us poor folks."

"Well, then maybe I'll be warmer than you in my cozy little garage." She shivered. "I wonder if it's always this cold over here. Although the scenery is gorgeous. All these rolling hills with cattle and sheep everywhere you look."

"Granny packed extra sweaters for me, so there's your answer."

"Oh, bother. I only brought one." She hurried up the steps next to Amanda. "How did the government get hold of this property?"

"It depends. Some of the rich folks have offered their places in order to control what they're used for, but most of the houses were requisitioned. I guess there's a list somewhere of all the big, old, fancy houses, and the government picked the ones they wanted then sent the owners packing."

"Is that fair?" Doris wrinkled her nose. "Where do the occupants go?"

Amanda shrugged. "There's a war on, so I guess it's what's best for the country. I'm not sure where the folks live now, but hopefully they're not too inconvenienced."

They entered the vast foyer, and Doris gasped. A shimmering crystal chandelier dangled from the twenty-foot ceiling, rainbow shards of light dancing across the mosaic tile floor. Nurses in dazzling white uniforms hurried through the massive foyer, their voices barely above a whisper.

An elderly nurse stood at the bottom of the stairs, hands clasped in front of her. "Welcome, ladies. I am Sister Greene, head nurse of this facility. You may stow your personal items behind the desk, then follow me. The nurses will follow me for a brief tour, and I will explain my expectations for you."

Doris leaned toward Amanda. "She's a nun?"

"No, silly. Nurses are called sisters over here."

"Oh. Thanks."

Sister Greene clapped her hands. "No talking, ladies. We have much to cover in a short time." She peered at them. "Which of you is Doris Strealer?"

Doris raised her hand.

"As an ambulance driver, there's no need for you to see the wards, so you are to report to the stables that have been converted to a garage where you will be trained in hospital procedures and driving techniques. It is unusual for hospitals to house their own ambulance, but the size and nature of our facility has called for this variance from normal protocols. Your services will also be shared with the dispatch facility, and a schedule will be worked out accordingly."

"Yes, ma'am. Where will I find the stables?"

"On the northeast corner of the estate." Sister Greene's gaze slid to Amanda and the other nurses, silently dismissing Doris.

"Thank you." Doris bowed at the retreating back of the head nurse then grinned at Amanda. "See you around, *sister.*" She shoved open the heavy wooden door and barreled into the firm chest of a white-coated figure. "Oh!" She stumbled backward. Strong hands grabbed her, and she regained her footing. "I'm sorry."

"This is a hospital. Please show some decorum."

Doris lifted her chin and glared at the doctor. "I apologized. There's no need to chop off my head."

He released her then stared down his nose, his piercing hazel-eyed gaze raking her from head to toe. "What are you doing here? Civilians are not allowed to visit."

Aware of her rumpled outfit and travel-weary appearance, she resisted the urge to smooth her hair and clothes for the condescending man. Just because he was a doctor, didn't mean he had the right to be rude. She crossed her arms. "I'm an ambulance driver with the Red Cross Motor Corps. Sister Greene sent me to find the garage. Not that I owe you any more of an explanation, but I'm thrilled to be here, and in my excitement I didn't pay attention. It won't happen again."

"Pertinent little thing, aren't you?"

Head cocked, she frowned up at the handsome physician who towered over her. Tall and good looking. She couldn't remember the last time she'd had to look up to a guy. Whoa, where had that thought come from? His height was irrelevant. She was there to work, not date.

"Look, I apologized and—" Her eyes widened, and she chuckled. "Wait a minute...I recognize you...I can't believe you're here. Not surprising that you've given me a tongue lashing for a minor infraction. You always were a bit pretentious. Sure, I'll straighten up, but you need to lighten up."

He puffed out his chest. "You can't speak to me like that, and I've never seen you before in my life."

"Yes, you have. I'm Doris Strealer, and you're Ronnie McCann. You were ahead of me in high school, a senior when I was a freshman. You used to bring your car to my father's garage before he sold it."

Ron's mouth gaped, and the air whooshed from his lungs. This statuesque, self-assured brunette was nothing like the gangly, brown-eyed teenager who had looked like a scarecrow in her oversized coveralls and a newsboy cap on her head. Visions of her hunched over the engine compartment of his car, wrench in hand and a grease streak on her cheek flitted through his mind. "How…why..."

Hands on her hips, she grinned. "At a loss for words, *Doctor* McCann? Well, that's a first."

He cleared his throat, his face warm. Since when did he blush? Good grief, the girl…er…woman would think him an imbecile. With his current behavior, she wouldn't be far off in her estimation. He swallowed. "We're in England. I didn't expect to run into anyone I know. You surprised me. That's all. Are you one of our new nurses?"

"Gracious me, no. I'm with the Red Cross Motor Corps. Driving ambulances for you and maintaining the vehicles."

"Driving for me?" He blinked. Why couldn't he think straight while standing in front of her? He really was a buffoon.

"Not for you personally. For the hospital." Her chocolate-brown eyes danced. "Unless, of course, you need some sort of chauffeur. Then

I'm your gal…well, once I get the hang of driving on the wrong side of the road."

"You're a smart one. I have no doubt about your abilities." Where had that come from? He barely knew the girl…woman. He needed to get away. She addled his brain. "Welcome to England, Miss Strealer. Glad to have you on board. Please excuse me. I must begin my rounds." He extended his arm, and she shook his hand. Soft, yet firm, her palm nestled in his. Tingles of electricity shot up to his elbow, and he pulled back as if stung.

Her smile faltered, and she shrugged. "See you around, Doc." She trotted down the steps and hurried across the meadow that separated the main house from the cottages and outbuildings.

Unable to tear away his gaze, he watched until she became a speck at the far end of the property. She been a cute teenager, but Doris Strealer had transformed into a beautiful woman. Beguiling brown eyes set above porcelain cheeks. Her hair gleamed even in the setting sun. He scrubbed at his face. She'd sure changed a lot in ten years, but he had, too.

No ring graced her left hand. Was it possible she was unmarried? Or did she refrain from wearing jewelry because of her work?

Ron shook his head. What did he care about her marital status? He was here to win the war against injuries and disease, and the gorgeous Miss Strealer would distract him from his mission. In another time and place, a distraction he would be glad of.

Chapter Three

Doris pulled a rag from the back pocket of her coveralls and wiped perspiration from her face. After a week of crummy weather, the sun had risen this morning in a cloudless sky. The brightness was a welcome change, but the temperature in the building was stifling. As of yet, no breeze swept through to cool the space.

After a final swipe at her face, she pocketed the cloth and shrugged. She'd worked in worse conditions. At least she was performing a job she loved. The other girls in the motor pool were swell, grease monkeys like her. All with similar stories of being unable to find garages that would hire them.

Several days of practice had given her the confidence to drive the ambulance on the left side of the road. Learning to operate the vehicle from the right seat and shifting with her left hand had been the most difficult challenge. She still periodically reached for the gear stick with the wrong hand and hit the door handle. Fortunately, no one was in the passenger seat to watch her make mistakes.

Especially the snooty Ron…Dr. McCann. Would she ever think of him that way? She'd seen him a few times from a distance, bringing back memories of crushing on him from across the cafeteria. Despite his arrogant behaviors in school, treating most people with disdain, she'd seen chinks in his armor that revealed an uncertain boy trying to prove his worth.

She blew out a breath. Puppy love and too many years ago to count.

"Hey, Doris. You almost finished with that truck? I've got to pick up supplies." Evelyn came around the corner, her uniform pressed and her hair pinned up under her cap. "I promised Nurse…uh…Sister Greene I'd get the stuff back by three o'clock."

"Don't you look slick?" Doris grinned. "You wouldn't be trying to catch the eye of a certain supply sergeant at the depot, would you?"

Face pink to the roots of her hair, Evelyn fanned herself. "And what if I was? You can't be jealous. I've seen how you eyeball our good doctor when you think no one is looking."

"Says you."

Evelyn giggled. "And Beatrice. And Maureen. And Lois. And—"

"All right. Enough of that. I'm just trying to figure him out. We went to high school together. I never figured him for going into medicine. Doesn't that require compassion? I haven't seen any evidence of those feelings."

"I heard two of the nurses talking. He'd gotten a reputation as a brilliant surgeon. His patients are unconscious. He doesn't have to show tenderness."

"Good point." Doris pointed at the engine with her wrench. "I have to reconnect the battery, and the vehicle is yours. Shouldn't take me but a few minutes." She eyed Evelyn in mock deference. "Stand back. We don't want you to mess up your outfit for the handsome sergeant."

"You're a peach."

She waved the tool. "Yeah, whatever." Bending over the engine, she hummed the latest Tommy Dorsey number.

"You're in a happy mood. What gives?"

"I've only been here for a week, but I feel more at home than…well, at home. I get to work on the vehicles, and no one looks at me weird or acts like my skills are unnatural. In fact, one of the new girls asked me to show her how to replace the solenoid. Felt good to be considered the expert for once, not some girl who is playing at auto mechanics. Doesn't that make you feel better about yourself?"

"I guess, although I've never worried about what others thought about me. If they're uncomfortable, it's their problem."

"I'm not sure that I care about what others think, but I applied at more than a dozen garages and service stations. Not one was willing to hire a woman, and they offered outrageous excuses. One guy had the audacity to say it would ruin his reputation as a serious mechanic." She grunted as she tightened the bolt, then stood back and appraised her work. Perfect. She slammed the hood and tossed the wrench into the metal toolbox with a clang. "Take that, Mr. Misogynistic Mechanic."

"Give 'em a break. This war has upended everything we used to know, and women doing men's jobs isn't what they're used to."

Doris scoffed. "Maybe they're afraid we'll be better than them. Whatever the reason, it's not fair that society dictates what we can or cannot do. America is provincial in its ideals, don't you think?"

"And the class system here in England isn't?" Evelyn held out her hand. "Gimme the keys. I've got to get a move on."

"They're inside the cab." She stepped away from the truck. "Be careful. With all the rain, the roads seem to have more potholes than usual. I don't want to have to do an alignment on this baby when you get back."

Evelyn snorted. "Liar. There's nothing you'd like better."

"Because the vehicles don't argue with me. What's not to like about them?" She gestured toward the doorway. "Off with you, now. Sergeant Steamy is waiting."

Giggling, Evelyn climbed into the truck. The engine roared to life, and she drove out of the garage.

Still smiling, Doris bent in front of her tool kit. Evelyn was a character. A whiz at tune-ups, her petite size enabled her to practically climb into the engine compartment to work. She was never without a smile and usually had an encouraging word for anyone she came into contact with. The only girl in a family of eight kids, she was an intriguing combination of rough-and-tumble and graceful.

Doris polished each wrench, screwdriver, and pair of pliers before tucking them in place. Just because she was a grease monkey didn't mean she was sloppy. Putting each item away ensured she could find her tools in a rush, kind of like a doctor with his scalpels during surgery. Ron's face came to mind, and she shook her head to get rid of the image.

As if she'd conjured him with her thoughts, he appeared in the doorway, a scowl on his face. "Are you the only driver available? I must get to London. There's a patient in need of my skills."

She gritted her teeth. Great. A two-hour drive with Dr. Difficult.

Ron pressed his lips together. Two hours trapped in an ambulance with Doris. What on earth would they talk about? With any luck, she'd be willing to make the trip in silence.

"I'd be happy to find another chauffeur for you, Dr. McCann." Doris's voice was void of emotion. "Let me check the schedule."

"No need." He waved his hand. "You'll do fine."

"Give me five minutes to change and sign out a vehicle." She pointed to a battered ambulance on the far side of the garage. "We'll take that one. An orderly can load any supplies required for the trip."

He held up his black leather satchel. "Everything I need is in here. I'll wait in the vehicle."

A curt nod, then she disappeared around the back of the vehicle. He opened the door and tucked his bag on the floor of the passenger side, then his gaze swept his surroundings. Tires were stacked in one corner. Rubber tubes and metal pieces of various shapes and sizes hung on the wall in what seemed to be a precise order. A metal box stood open on the floor. Inside, each gleaming tool nestled in a slot carved into a slab of wood. What sort of person did that?

Someone as organized and fastidious about their work implements as he was. Since Doris was the only mechanic in the building, the tool chest must be hers. He shook his head. There was more to her than met the eye. He bent and latched the lid, then grasped the handle and hefted the box onto one of the vacant counters that lined the walls.

He grunted at the weight of the box. Surely, she didn't carry this thing on her own. He brushed off his hands and climbed into the front of the ambulance, closing the door with a bang that echoed in the cavernous space.

Before he could wonder when she would return, Doris yanked open the driver's side door and slid behind the wheel. Without a glance, she started the engine and pulled out of the building. The vehicle bumped and rocked over the gravel lane that led to the main road.

From the corner of his eye, he watched her handle the oversized steering wheel, her posture relaxed and confident. With fluid motions, she guided the truck around the dips and holes that littered the macadam. Intent on her task, she seemed oblivious to his presence.

A mahogany-colored tendril escaped from under her visored cap, and his fingers itched to tuck the strand behind her ear where the curve of her neck disappeared into the collar of her uniform. He blinked. Where had that thought come from? They had a job to do. Nothing more.

He swallowed, then coughed.

One hand still on the wheel, she reached behind the seat and pulled out a canteen. "Help yourself."

"When did you load this into the vehicle?"

"This morning. I ensure there's fresh water in all the ambulances each day." She shrugged. "Canteens are also checked after each trip."

"I never would have thought to do that." He put the vessel to his lips and drank, the liquid tepid but soothing to his dry throat. "You seem to run a tight operation."

A smirk tugged at the corner of her mouth. "We girls aren't totally useless, then?"

"Hey, I—"

Her laugh filled the cab, and he grinned. "Funny."

"I thought so." She sobered up. "So what made you go into medicine? I thought you were on track to be an accountant or something like that."

"I went into college intending to obtain a business degree, but then I took a biology class for my science elective, and I was hooked. The more I learned, the more I wanted to know. In my sophomore year, I changed majors. It's been a good fit."

"Word is you're brilliant. Any truth to that?"

"I seem to have a knack for surgery. It's dangerous to listen to the kudos, too easy to become arrogant."

"Where's the pretentious guy who reprimanded me on the stairs?"

He grinned. "I gave him the day off."

She guffawed then covered her mouth with one hand. Her cheeks pinked.

Ron chuckled. He enjoyed her laugh, full of joy and abandonment. He'd have to figure out a way to make her laugh more often. He liked the way it sounded and how it made him believe there wasn't a care in the world. "My turn to ask questions. Where did you learn to be an ace mechanic?"

"My dad." Her eyes took on a distant look. "When I was around ten years old, Mom dropped off my younger sister Emily and me at his place because she had to go somewhere with my sister Cora. He let me hold the flashlight and hand him tools, probably to keep me out of trouble, but I was fascinated by how the pieces were assembled. I loved seeing him change a broken or rusted piece with a shiny, new replacement."

She sighed. "It wasn't long before I was stopping there every day after school. I picked up a lot just by watching him, but as I got older, he taught me how to do everything from changing the oil to replacing gaskets on the engine block. Mom was less than thrilled at first, but I guess she and Dad finally got used to the idea. Maybe they thought I'd grow out of it."

"And now you're fixing cars in England."

"I—"

In the distance, an airplane engine buzzed, and Ron peeked out the window. The aircraft approached. He squinted into the glare then gulped.

On the bottom of each wing was painted the black, crooked cross of the German Luftwaffe. "Stop the ambulance. Get out. It's a bomber."

Doris slammed on the brakes then turned off the engine. She shoved open the door and leapt out.

Ron jumped out of the ambulance and pointed to the nearest hedgerow.

The V1 shrieked, its strident whistle shattering the afternoon.

They raced toward the thicket. She began to lag, and he wrapped his arm around her shoulder, pulling her with him. Eyes wide, she nodded her thanks. They dove underneath the shrubbery. He shielded her with his body, her warmth permeating his shirt.

Somewhere deep in the woods on the other side of the road, the bomb exploded. The sound of trees snapping and crashing to the forest floor filled the air. The ground beneath them rumbled. Then silence.

Ron looked over his shoulder. The sky was clear of aircraft, but the acrid smell of smoldering wood clung to the breeze. He coughed and staggered to his feet. He held out his hand to Doris. "Are you all right? That was a close one."

Face wan, she nodded then scrambled off the ground. Knocking the dirt from her uniform, she scraped her hair from her eyes. "I've lost my hat somewhere."

Even disheveled she was beautiful. He smiled. "We should go back to the hospital and report the bombing. Perhaps get one of the orderlies to drive me."

Her eyebrow quirked. "Nonsense. Anyone in a five-mile radius knows about the bombing, and I'm perfectly capable of getting you to London." Her voice shook, and she cleared her throat then lifted her chin. "Time's wasting. Let's go." She strode through the brush toward the ambulance.

He shook his head. Adrenaline surged through him, and his heart thundered in staccato beats. Surely, Doris felt the same anxiety, yet she'd stalked across the meadow, determined to finish her task. Did she realize how unique she was?

Chapter Four

A cacophony of voices mingled with the sound of silverware scraping on china. Doris nibbled at the warm, yeasty roll letting the conversations wash over her. The girls seemed giddy tonight, but the only emotion she could work up was disappointment. She and Ron finished the mission after the bombing without further incident. He'd been solicitous and kind, but the overbearing streak she'd seen seemed to have disappeared. He was almost likable.

They talked about everything and nothing on the return trip, then she'd billeted at the dispatch facility for the last three days per her agreement. Was the Red Cross so short of women they had to spread workers over multiple locations? Learning two sets of rules under different supervisors wasn't difficult, but it did make her job a challenge.

When she arrived this morning to report to Sister Greene, Ron had been conducting rounds in the ward. She'd waved at him across the ballroom-dormitory, but he hadn't returned the greeting. Had she broken some unspoken code of conduct, or did he regret being nice to her?

"Doris got to drive him over to London last week. That must have been a nightmare." Maureen poked her ribs. "You going to give us the skinny?"

"I'm sorry, what?" Doris blinked and looked at Maureen.

"What do you think of Dr. McCann? I heard the two of you missed being bombed by a hairsbreadth. Too bad you weren't able to cozy up in some Anderson shelter."

"The Jerry must need cheaters. He missed us by a long shot. Did you find out where he came from? Kind of odd getting attacked by one plane."

"Nobody's talking. Maybe he got lost." Maureen laid down her fork with a clatter. "What gives? You gonna tell us about Dr. Dreamboat or not?"

"There's nothing to tell."

"I heard you used to go to school together."

Doris tore off a hunk of bread and popped it in her mouth. Chewing slowly, she shook her head.

Lois giggled. "You're stalling. I think he's fantastic. Intelligent and good looking."

"Too much of a brooding Mr. Rochester-type for me, girls." Maureen wiggled her eyebrows. "I'll take Dr. O'Hare instead."

"Been reading *Jane Eyre* again?" Lois cocked her head.

"Why not? It's my favorite. You've got to admit I'm right, Doris. While you were gone, he yelled at Amanda for being slow during surgery, then he nearly took my head off yesterday, claiming I'd brought him the wrong supplies." She frowned. "But I didn't. Even if I had, he had no call to be so rude."

She shrugged. So much for turning the conversation away from the handsome physician. "Look, I barely know him. He was three years ahead of me and did not fraternize with freshmen."

"And now?" Lois peered at her.

"Now what?"

"You spent hours with him. Certainly, you know a bit more about him."

"You'd make a great war correspondent digging for details." She folded her hands. "Fine. Here's what I know. He graduated from Dartmouth. A couple of weeks after he finished his residency at Massachusetts General, he got drafted. He has no hobbies as far as I know, but he does like football." She stuck out her tongue at Maureen. "Satisfied?"

"Not quite, but the information is a start. One of the new nurses said the other doctors can't stand him, but their attitude is probably professional jealousy. He is the best, from what I understand. At least that's what Sister Greene says. She seems to be president of his fan club."

"And only member." Lois snorted a laugh.

"No need to be mean." Doris stabbed at a carrot on her plate. "The man has standards. What's wrong with that? We're all here to do a job, not make new friends. He's saved more than his fair share of young men from death and dismemberment in the short time I've been here. I'd say that counts for a little respect. And if he's not the warmest of human beings, so be it."

"Oooh, you're defending him. There must be something going on."

"Stop being a knucklehead, Maureen." Doris shook her head and continued to poke at her food. She'd never let the abrasive girl know she'd hit a nerve. Why did Ron have to be so attractive on the outside yet not so much on the inside? There had been a glimmer of niceness during the trip, yet the girls made it sound like he'd been an ogre while she was away. Good thing she didn't have to work with him on a regular basis. She'd stay in the garage with vehicles that weren't nearly as difficult to understand.

———◆———

Ron whistled Glenn Miller's "That Old Black Magic" and tapped on the steering wheel in rhythm to the music. The day dawned damp and gloomy, but blue sky began to peek from amid the gray clouds. Meeting in London with other Army Medical Corps hospital directors had been stimulating and encouraging. The opportunity to spend time with other professionals in the industry to debate the pros and cons of new advances made up for the drudgery of running the facility that required the submission of endless forms and reports.

He glanced out the window and slowed the jeep to enjoy the picturesque sight of a cluster of farm buildings and cows grazing in the distance. Unfamiliar birdsong emanated from the copse of trees along the road. Lush and green, the meadow to his left was perfect for a picnic.

Doris's face sprang to mind, and he sighed. He hadn't spoken to her since her return from dispatch. Sure, their jobs kept them both busy, but she wasn't at lunch or dinner the day before he left. Did engine repair and maintenance take so long that she didn't have time for meals? He stroked the seat next to him. Had she done the work on this jeep?

Perhaps he should thank her. He grinned. Giving her a compliment was sure to confuse her. Thus far, their interaction had been a combination of meandering down memory lane and debating some social issue. High spirited and feisty, she was an intelligent partner to spar with. His stomach rumbled, and he accelerated the vehicle. If he hurried, he could catch her before dinner started.

Throat dry, he coughed then snapped his fingers and reached behind the seat. Ah, there it is. His hand wrapped around the canteen, and he pulled out the vessel. Shaking it, he smiled. Full, thanks to Doris. He unscrewed the lid and took a long draft. Who knew tepid water from a metal canister could revive a man?

The scenery whizzed past as he zipped down the road. He downshifted around a curve then sped up again like a horse who knows the barn isn't far. Since when did he know anything about farm animals? Sure, Dartmouth College sat on the banks of the Connecticut River in rural New Hampshire, but he'd not wandered the granite hills enough to familiarize himself with the agrarian society surrounding the school. Competition to graduate with honors was fierce, leaving no time for leisure activities.

The earthy smell of freshly turned soil and manure peppered the air. He wrinkled his nose. The antiseptic aroma of bleach was more to his liking. Crisp. Clean. Much better.

Ron glanced at his watch. Another four or five miles to go. A long but easy trip. Another swig of water, then he closed the cap and tucked the canteen between the seats.

A gasp, then a moan from the engine, then nothing. Not a sound from under the hood. The gauge claimed he had a quarter tank of fuel, so he'd not been stupid enough to run out of gas. He steered the jeep to the side of the road and twisted the key in the ignition. Off. On. Off. On.

Silence.

With a growl, he slammed his palms on the dashboard. He shoved open the door and crawled out. Standing beside the traitorous vehicle, he rubbed his jaw and frowned. What he knew about motors fit on a dust speck. Should he try to diagnose the problem or start walking in order to get back before dark?

He popped the hood and looked inside the engine compartment. Wires snaked between the parts. Memories of the few times his father had tried to teach him the basics of auto mechanics flooded his mind. Thinking the skills unnecessary, Ron hadn't bothered to pay close attention. He raked his fingers through his hair then touched the cap on the radiator burning his fingers. Idiot. Of course the components were hot.

"Face it, McCann, you're out of your league here and hiking back to the hospital." He blew out a breath then ducked into the jeep for his satchel and grabbed the canteen. Would Doris be angry that he removed it from the vehicle? He frowned. What did her mood matter? She was at fault for the dead jeep.

"Hey, there! Everything okay?"

Still inside the jeep, he'd know her voice anywhere. What was Doris doing out and about? He left the items in the vehicle and turned.

Doris braked the red-and-white Hiawatha bicycle and gaped at him. "Ron...er...Dr. McCann...is there a problem?"

"No, I'd had enough driving, so I thought I'd walk the rest of the trip, stretch my legs."

Her face reddened, and she dismounted without a word.

He flinched. His frustration didn't warrant incivility. Why did her presence often bring out the rough side of his tongue?

She laid the bike on its side then sauntered to the front of the jeep and leaned inside the engine compartment.

Did she have no sense of urgency? He watched as she checked connections, a look of concentration on her face. After several minutes, she shook her head and grabbed a small metal box from the back of the jeep. Of course she kept tools in each of the vehicles. Not that he would have known what to do with them. "What's wrong with the vehicle? Do you think you can fix the problem?

"I'm not sure and probably." She popped open the box and withdrew a flashlight that she handed to him. "Make yourself useful, and shine this where I tell you to." Grabbing a couple of wrenches and a screwdriver, she returned to the engine. "Are you coming?"

He'd been caught staring. "Yes, sorry." He hurried toward her and clicked on the light. "Ready."

"Good." She climbed onto the bumper and reached deep into the engine. After a few grunts, she waved the wrench. "Try it now."

He trotted to the driver's side and turned the key. The engine sputtered then roared to life. He grinned. She was a lifesaver.

She jumped to the ground and closed the hood with a bang then tossed the tools into the metal box. She brushed off her hands then picked up the box and returned it to the jeep. "You shouldn't have any more problems." Uprighting her bike, she gripped the handlebars.

"I…uh…thank you."

Touching two fingers to her forehead in mock salute, she shrugged. "You're welcome. When I get back, I'll give the vehicle a once-over. See if I can't prevent this from happening again."

"You're very proficient at this. Smart, too. Don't you want to be more than a mechanic? You could be a nurse or a teacher or anything you wanted."

Her face darkened. "Because only dumb people are interested in cars, Doctor? I see you haven't changed since high school. Still judging people and thinking you're better than everyone else. For your information, I can't be anything I want because men hold all the cards in employment. Women are doing men's work now, but we will be expected to shuffle home quietly when the boys return." She hopped on the bike and pedaled away.

Ron sighed. Even in slacks with smudges on her face, she's feminine, but why does she enjoy doing masculine work? If they were married, he'd never let her hold such a job. A vision of Doris standing in front of a stove wearing coveralls flashed into his head, and he chuckled. She was getting under his skin, and that was a problem.

Chapter Five

In the growing darkness, Doris peered at her watch. Her stomach complained, confirming that she'd missed dinner because of having to pick up Dr. Difficult from the train station after his trip to Liverpool. An awkward silence permeated the journey, and she pressed her lips together to prevent saying something she might regret later. Ron made it clear he was in no mood for conversation, speaking in clipped sentences when she asked how his patients were faring.

Should she try to get another assignment? She was tired of walking on eggshells for the man. No. He would not win this competition. She huffed out a sigh, and he glanced at her, eyebrows raised in question.

The jeep did its typical shimmy and bumping along the road, jostling her into Ron's shoulder. "Sorry. She righted her uniform cap and took a tighter grip on the steering wheel.

"Do you have to hit every crevice in the street?"

"Actually, I've managed to miss a few." She let sarcasm infiltrate her words. "But I'd be happy to let you drive, if you'd prefer, Dr. McCann."

"We're almost there."

"Otherwise, you'd take over?"

"Look—"

An air raid siren wailed, its strident tones carrying across the rolling hills from the hospital. A chill swept over Doris. Only a few days had passed since the last incident. Bombing raids were discussed at length during her orientation, but she'd been foolish enough to believe she could handle the Jerries and their air assaults. Her gaze shot to Ron. "Would you like me to try to make it to the hospital?"

He leaned out the window. "Yes, its cellar is our best chance for safe shelter."

She clenched the wheel and pressed the accelerator. The jeep bucked like an unbroken horse and bounced through a deep hole, lifting her from the seat. Her breath hitched. Get hold of yourself, girl. The doctor would not be impressed if you panicked. *God, please keep us safe.* She peered through the windshield. Nothing. Then the familiar buzz of approaching planes sounded in the distance.

Tiny black specks appeared in the sky. A squadron, rather than a one-off like last time. The number of planes didn't bode well. What was their target? She slammed her foot on the brake and doused the headlights. "I'm not taking any chances the pilots can see us, even from that height."

"Agreed. We should make a run for it." Ron picked up his doctor's bag and pushed open the door. "Under the trees or in the culvert?"

"Culvert." She killed the engine and jumped from the vehicle. Clamping her hand on her hat, she dashed toward the earthen channel that lined the road.

He grabbed her hand and dragged her away from the vehicle. "In case they can see us, we shouldn't hide near the jeep."

They ran about thirty yards down the road. The whining whistle of the bomb pierced the air, and he pushed her into the trench.

Doris stumbled and rolled into the bottom with a grunt. She curled into a ball and covered her head with her arms. Ron curved his frame over hers as he had done during last week's event. His warm closeness sent tingles snaking up her spine. What was wrong with her? They could be dead in the next minute, yet her traitorous body betrayed her with its response. She squeezed her eyes closed. "Please, God, let the Jerries miss us and anyone else they might be aiming for. The Lord is my Shepherd, I shall not want. He—"

"…leadeth me beside the still waters." Ron's baritone voice joined hers.

Her eyes shot open. His face was inches from hers, and she searched his face in the dimness. "Since when do you quote Scripture?"

"Since I turned my life over to God at university." A smile quirked the corner of his mouth. "Surprised, are you?"

"Yeah, I guess so. You're so confident about your abilities, I…uh…" She dropped her gaze.

"You mean arrogant." He sighed. "Even as a believer I struggle with pride. Medicine comes easy for me, which gives me self-assurance. The attitude often is perceived as hubris."

"Maybe, but right now I appreciate your certainty. Those planes are terrifying, yet you seem unaffected by them."

"Appearances can be deceiving, but in this case, I think we're safe. Their trajectory is wrong for the hospital. Unfortunately, the fleet may be heading to the munitions factory. We must pray the enemy misses their target, whatever it may be."

"Please, God," Doris whispered.

The airplanes' hum faded, then a series of muffled explosions resonated in the blackness. Ron's eyes closed for a brief moment, sorrow etched on his face. With a sigh, he crawled off her, then rose. Even though the day's heat clung to the night air, the absence of his form chilled her.

He grasped her hand and pulled her to her feet then wrapped his arm around her shoulder and led her out of the gully. "We're safe now. Let's get to the hospital. Perhaps by the time we arrive, reports about the bombing will be available."

She trembled at his touch as they picked their way to the jeep.

"Are you cold?"

"No, still a bit wobbly." Good thing he couldn't see her face. Beet red, if the amount of heat she felt was an indicator. He'd also see she was lying.

He pulled her closer. "Of course. You were very brave."

Doris shook her head. "Maybe on the outside…" But definitely not on the inside. They climbed into the vehicle and were soon on their way. The earlier discomfort between them was gone. She shook her head.

Apparently, life-threatening events were necessary to building their friendship. "You told me why you got into medicine, but why do you stay in it? What do you love about the field?"

"No one has ever asked me that before." He looked off into the distance. "Human anatomy is a mystery. The way our systems respond to injury and illness. We doctors only do so much with our techniques, whether surgery or pharmaceuticals, then the body takes over to heal and repair itself. I learn something new every day, which is exciting.

"You make yourself sound not much more than a mechanic."

He shrugged. "God is the one who saves. I'm merely his instrument."

She blinked. Confident yet humble, the man was an enigma. An alluring mystery she'd love to solve.

———————◆———————

Ron gripped the door handle as the jeep rattled over the washboard road. He peeked at Doris, who hunched over the wheel, eyes intent on their destination. She swerved, and he jostled her arm. She glanced at him. "Sorry."

He smiled. "You're doing fine." Only minutes earlier, they'd been arguing about her driving. Now, he appreciated her calm determination driving in less-than-ideal conditions. Most women he knew sat in the back of a chauffeur-driven sedan oblivious to the inner workings of the car or the challenge of navigating the highways. He cleared his throat. "My turn to ask questions. You told me why you're a mechanic. What do you love about it?"

"Don't you really mean why didn't I choose nursing or teaching?" She grinned, taking the sting from her words.

"Yeah, about that—"

"Forget about it." She waved her hand. "My relationship with auto mechanics is complicated. Spending time with my dad was special. We could talk about anything as long as we were stooped over an engine or lying on the ground under a chassis. Working with him taught me the patience and skills to diagnose a problem."

"But that's not the complication, is it?"

She gave him a sidelong glance. "No. Being a grease monkey made me different from the other girls. I wasn't interested in clothes or shopping or dreaming about movie stars. Being tall and gangly didn't help either. Most of the guys were shorter than me—still are. I wasn't considered girly enough for the kids."

His heart constricted. "Were you taunted?"

"Teenage girls can be ruthless. I preferred the times they ignored me."

He patted her shoulder, the warmth of her body permeating the fabric under his palm. He pulled away and laced his fingers. "Too bad people aren't as easy to analyze as cars, huh?"

"Exactly! I considered trying to change so the girls would like me, but Dad convinced me I didn't want those kinds of people as friends."

"Wise man."

"Maybe, but I still struggled with insecurity throughout high school." She sighed. "I'm not sure why I'm telling you all this."

"Because I asked. Remember?"

"Right. Anyway, I tried a year of college but was miserable. Dad let me drop out and work at his garage…the happiest time of my life. But his health took a turn, and he sold the business. None of the other places in town would hire me."

He cringed. No wonder she reacted with anger when he spouted his opinions about her vocation. Had the female medical students and residents had the same sorts of difficulties? He'd been so focused on his own career, he'd never noticed. *Forgive me, Lord.*

"The thing about cars and engines is their predictability. Each vehicle is designed using specific parts with definitive purposes that can only be assembled one way. Predictability is comfortable. People are…you know…"

"Unpredictable, and therefore uncomfortable."

"Yeah, very."

"How about the girls in the motor corps? Do you get along?"

"For the most part. We have a couple of gals…well…uh…"

"Who make it feel like high school all over again?"

She giggled, bell-like. "Something like that."

His heart warmed. Her classmates were wrong. She was definitely girly.

The Mechanic and The MD   46

Chapter Six

Rain pummeled the windshield, and the wipers struggled to clear the sheets of water. Thunder boomed overhead. Doris gripped the steering wheel, her knuckles white. A frog strangler, as her aunt would say. The taillights of the ambulance in front of her were barely visible through the torrent. *Lord, please don't let me drive into a tree.* She licked her dry lips. Must remember to breathe.

Next to her, Maureen kept up a constant stream of chatter. Did the woman not care about the four patients in the back of the ambulance? All Doris could think about was the horrific injuries on their bodies. Fortunately, no one died as a result of the explosion at the munitions factory. Yet. The desire to get the victims into Ron's capable hands warred with the necessity of not worsening their wounds by jostling them over the uneven roads.

"I hate what the weather does to my hair, don't you? I'll be a frizzled mess by the time we get back." Maureen frowned and fiddled with her unruly hair. "You have it easy with those straight locks of yours. Just tuck 'em under your cap and go."

They were on a mission of life and death, and all the woman could care about was how she looked. Doris rolled her eyes. What kind of person does that?

Show her grace, My child. As I have done for you.

Guilt pricked Doris, and she sighed, searching her mind for something to say that wouldn't sound like a criticism. She mumbled an incoherent response that could be taken as affirmation.

The storm abated, and Doris swiveled her neck to unknot the muscles in her shoulder. Clothes damp from loading the patients during the worst of the downpour, her uniform clung to her skin. How long before she could peel off the wet garments, climb into her pajamas, and nestle under the covers?

Maureen continued to prattle. "I thought if I worked for the Red Cross, I'd spend more time with the doctors or at least the medics. This driving up and down the roads in the backwoods of England is tedious. Don't you think?"

"No. I like driving, and I especially enjoy working on the vehicles."

"I like that, too, but we're stuck in the garage for hours at a time."

"We're mechanics with the motor corps." Doris glanced at her passenger. "What did you expect?"

With a shrug, Maureen inspected her fingernails. "The recruiting officer made the job sound glamorous, but so far the closest I've gotten to glamour is on my nights off when I can give myself a manicure and a pedicure. I want to end up with a husband after all this suffering, you know? And if he happens to be a rich doctor, so much the better. But I don't want to settle down right away. Life's too short, especially here, where we have to worry about being bombed."

"The raids do make our lives more precarious, but the uncertainty has given me a greater appreciation for each moment."

"Exactly! I plan to jam as much fun into every minute as I can. The wine isn't that great, but the music, dancing, and ratio of guys to gals is a decent substitute. If I'm going to die, I'm going to savor each day as if it's my last."

Doris took a deep breath. She didn't want to offend Maureen, but she needed to understand the futility of her hedonistic lifestyle. "But what about after you die? Are you prepared for what comes next?"

Maureen wrinkled her nose. "Nothing comes next. We live. We die. Poof. Then nothing."

"I believe differently. May I tell you about it?"

"You've no right to judge me and my decisions. I've heard about you. How straitlaced you are."

"I'm not judging you, but I'd like to give you some information to consider."

"Fine." Maureen flounced against the seat and crossed her arms. "But I'm not making any promises."

"According to the Bible—"

"A bunch of fairy tales."

"There are many secular scholars who wrote about the events that are recorded in the Bible, including Jesus' life. And He said many times there is life after death, and we have an opportunity to be in heaven with Him and His Father after we die. Life is hard, especially now, but I'm able to have peace about my circumstances because of my belief in Him."

"So you never get upset?"

Doris held up her hand. "Just the opposite. Unfortunately, I have a temper, and my knee-jerk reactions and mouth often put me in hot water, but when I remember to ask for God's help in situations, I'm able to deal with them a lot better."

"But don't you want to have fun?"

"Absolutely. But I want my amusement to come without regrets."

Maureen's face pinked. "Yeah, I've got plenty of those. But it's too late for me to start over."

"No. You can begin anew at any time with God. He doesn't have a deadline."

The gates of the hospital appeared, and Doris frowned. Who knew she'd be disappointed to arrive at their destination? She needed more time to explain.

Patience, child. You've planted a seed.

She braked the ambulance behind the other vehicles. Orderlies and nurses rushed patients into the building. "We better get hopping, but anytime you want to talk, I'm available."

"Okay. You've given me a lot to think about. Thanks for not getting mad when I said some of those things."

Doris nodded.

They jumped out and hurried to open the back of the ambulance. Maureen climbed inside, grabbed one end of the first stretcher, and then moved the wounded into the cavernous entryway of the hospital. Lined up along the walls, the patients waited their turns in the operating room.

At one end of the room, Ron knelt beside a man who moaned and held his bandaged head. The doctor's words were unintelligible, but calm assurance exuded from his posture and kind smile on his face. Doris stared at him for a long moment.

Maureen poked her in the ribs. "I'm sure you'd like to spend all day watching Dr. Dreamboat, but there are three more stretchers to retrieve."

"Right." Doris slapped her forehead. "He was…I just…never mind."

With a smirk, Maureen hooked her hand through Doris's arm. "You can tell me all about it while we work."

"There's nothing to say."

"I don't believe you, but we've got work to do so I won't push you, but later…" She gave Doris a cheeky grin and waggled her eyebrows. "I want the lowdown on the good doctor."

Doris's face warmed, and she ducked her head.

"Now, I know there's something." She laughed. "And Strealer, don't ever play poker."

They finished moving the patients, and Doris headed to the driver's side to stow the ambulance in the garage.

"Miss Strealer, putting away the vehicle can wait." Ron stood on the pillared verandah, a clipboard in hand. "You're needed in triage."

"I'm not a nurse."

"But as a member of the Red Cross, you've had basic first-aid training. There are three nurses down with the flu, and Sister Greene is managing the operating room, which is where I should be. You are capable of performing basic assessments. And this isn't a request, it's an order."

She pressed her lips together. The arrogant doctor was back in business. With a mock salute, she trotted up the stairs. "Yes, sir. Where should I begin?"

He pointed to the far end of the foyer. "The last man in the corner. To review your responsibilities, take only sixty to ninety seconds to make your assessment. Is breathing labored? Does the airway seem impaired? What is the skin color and moisture level? Check the pulse speed and rhythm and level of consciousness." He handed her a stack of tags and a pencil. "Mark the information on these, and tie the tag to a button or some part of the clothing. One of the junior cadet nurses will put patients in order of priority. Understood?"

"Yes." She clutched the cards in cold hands. Would someone die because she failed?

Ron lifted her chin with his finger until her eyes met his. "You can do this. Don't second-guess yourself. I'll be over there if you need me." He ran his knuckle along her jaw then pivoted on his heel and strode to the far side of the room.

She shivered, and her skin tingled where he'd touched her. One minute bossy and the next encouraging. Her emotions got a case of whiplash when she was around him. She needed to spend more time in the garage. Chest tight, she gripped the pencil and picked her way through the stretchers to her first patient.

What did she care how Ron acted? He would never be interested in someone like her: a girl who hadn't finished college and got grease under her nails. Besides, there was a war on. No one in their right mind got involved in a serious relationship. Either one of them could be killed at any time. Their near misses during the bombing raids had proven that fact.

Ron's voice carried toward her. She resisted the urge to turn and watch him, but an image of his face flashed into her mind anyway. His intriguing hazel eyes with crinkles around the edges and his athletic build. Since when did doctors come in such hunky packages? Every shred of willpower would be necessary to focus on the job. Maybe she should put in for a transfer to a location where the doctors weren't so enticing.

Chapter Seven

Ron eyed Doris as she made her way from stretcher to stretcher, her pale face determined yet compassionate. Pencil gripped between her fingers, she examined each patient with a studied gaze, then she made notations on the tags. With a smile and a quiet word, she moved on to the next victim. He glanced at his watch. She averaged two-and-a-half minutes with each man. Not bad for a first-timer.

"Am I going to lose my leg, Doctor?"

Ron gazed down at the soldier lying on the floor, his freckles dark against his ashen skin. The boy's uniform was dirty and torn, his white bandages in stark contrast. "I can't make any promises other than I will do my best to ensure you'll be dancing on your wedding day. How does that sound?"

The young man grinned, then grimaced, and clutched his side. "I think I mighta broke my ribs, Doc. Can you take a look at them?"

"I'll be sure to check you from tip to toe." He tied the tag to the soldier's uniform then patted his shoulder. It was dangerous to get chummy with the patients in case they didn't live, but surely he could patch up this boy as good as new. "Close your eyes and rest."

"Thanks, Doc. Take good care of my buddy, too, will ya?"

"Absolutely. We only offer the best service." Ron rose, his knees protesting the sudden motion. He swayed, and a small hand steadied him from behind. He gained his balance and turned.

Expression wary, Doris stood, one arm outstretched, the other tucked to her side gripping the clipboard. "I've finished with the group of patients along the far wall. Would you like me to take over here so you can get into the operating theater?"

"Not just yet. I'd like to check your work."

Her lips thinned then relaxed. "Of course. My first assignment as triage nurse." Her eyes sparkled with suppressed laughter. "Although in this getup, it's a wonder the boys didn't object to my ministrations. I'm missing that cute seersucker uniform with the jaunty hat."

"You don't need any particular outfit to look cute." He winked then held his breath. He'd not meant to blurt out his thoughts. Would she be offended at the off-the-cuff comment?

"Thanks for that, but I'm sure you're just being kind." She swept her arm toward the line of patients. "Lay on, MacDuff."

He chuckled. "Ah, a Shakespearean student. You obviously know that line is often misquoted."

"I'm not just another pretty face, Doctor." She batted her eyes and mugged a pinup pose. "I've got brains, too."

"Of that I'm sure." Still grinning, he walked to the litters and quickly reviewed her assessments. Impressive. Her handwriting was neat and readable, the information concise and correct. "Well done, Miss Strealer. You may have found a new calling."

Her cheeks flushed, and she dropped her gaze. "I'll stick to cars, thank you."

"Not yet. There are a handful of patients yet to appraise, then I'll need you to follow me into surgery."

"I beg your pardon?" Her eyes were so wide, her deep brown irises swam in a sea of white.

"As I said, I'm down three nurses, and the orderlies have their own responsibilities. After we're done here, we'll scrub up, and you'll assist me in the operating room."

The color drained from her face in a flash, and she gulped. "But—"

"I won't let you fail." He curved his lips into what he hoped was an encouraging smile. "Now, *MacBeth*, let's hop to it."

Suspicion clinging to her expression, she nodded and took a deep breath.

They squatted near the first of the remaining patients, and he cocked his head. "What is your appraisal, Miss Strealer?"

"Uh, okay, patient is conscious and alert; his color is good, airway is not blocked, and"—she pressed her index and middle fingers against the inside of the man's wrist—"pulse is steady and strong. His arm is splinted, therefore the medics feel the limb may be broken."

"Very good. I will confirm their theory later, but he should be fine until we can get to him." Ron reached for the tag on which she'd made notations, and their fingers brushed. Electricity shot up his arm, and his heart rate jumped. His adrenaline surged. He failed on willing his hands not to tremble like a schoolboy's with his first crush. If he didn't get a handle on the attraction he felt when Doris was nearby, the patients might suffer, which he couldn't allow.

She was nothing like the women he'd dated. Not that there had been many. He'd been so focused on completing his education and starting his career, he'd had very little personal life. He'd also had no interest in the female med students. They were competitors, not marriage material. The few gals he'd walked out with during college were petite and perky, and hung on his every word. Granted, that was before they got to know him. Within weeks of their first dinner, they would break off the relationship, citing his self-absorption and arrogance.

Ron wended his way through the corridor to the parlor-surgical suite, Doris by his side. She walked to the corner of the room where a sink had been installed after the Medical Corps arrived. Wasn't confidence necessary in medicine? Doctors, especially surgeons, can't waffle on their decisions. Insecure physicians make mistakes, and errors are unacceptable.

She hunched over the basin scrubbing her hands and arms up to her elbows. Sharp as a tack, she questioned his motives, had strong opinions that opposed his own, and her behavior turned societal expectations upside down. Definitely not what the doctor ordered.

He waited until she was finished before washing his own hands then jerked his head toward the nearest gurney that held a patient. An anesthesiologist sat at the man's head and had already rendered the man unconscious. A nurse hurried to them and pulled their white cotton surgical masks over their nose and mouth.

Doris's eyebrows almost reached her hairline, and her eyes darted from the patient to the tray of gleaming instruments then to his face.

"Relax. Look at me." He waited until her gaze came to rest on his face. "Excellent. An operating room can get noisy, but I'm the only thing you should focus on. Try to tune out everything but this space that is your whole world right now. I will point to each item as I need it. Your job is to pick up whatever I've indicated with haste and slap it into my palm. Clear?"

Mute, she nodded, eyes glistening.

The poor woman was obviously terrified, yet she remained at his side, ready to assist. Not all nurses were cut out to be in the OR, and Doris hadn't signed up for this. She had pluck. He'd give her that.

A glance from the anesthesiologist told him the patient was ready. With his gloved pinky finger, he pointed to the scalpel. "Scalpel."

Doris fumbled the metal lancet, dropping it onto the floor with a clatter. "I'm so sorry."

"You're fine. We have plenty. Try again with the one that was next to it."

She nodded and picked up the second scalpel then slapped it into his palm.

Hand stinging from the force of the blow, his fingers wrapped around the handle. He cut into the patient's leg, and Doris gasped. She swayed, nearly bumping his shoulder. Was he going to lose her before the procedure?

"Doris?"

"Fine. I'm fine." She took a deep breath, her mask buckling. She straightened her spine and met his gaze. "I promise."

"Good girl."

Incisions made, he held out his hand. "Clamp. And go easy on me."

"Clamp." She pressed the instrument into his palm and grinned. "Was that better?"

"Much. Can't injure the surgeon now, can we?"

She giggled, and he smiled. Her shoulders were no longer hiked up to her ears. Perhaps, she was beginning to calm down.

Hours passed, and he lost track of the time. Victim after victim was placed in front of him until the bodies blurred into one. Doris never flagged in her assistance, although as the day wore on, lines appeared on her face, and her back began to curve. Exhaustion was obvious with her every movement.

A pair of orderlies whisked away the latest soldier, and he looked toward the vacant doorway. Sister Greene leaned against the frame. "That was the last of them."

With a sigh, he massaged his neck, muscles stiff and unbending. Stripping off his gloves, he tossed them onto the tray of instruments. "Congratulations, Miss Strealer, you survived your first fourteen-hour surgical shift. Well done."

Doris tugged off her mask, and a wan smile barely lifted her lips. "Thank you, sir." She began to untie the straps on the gown covering her uniform, then her eyes rolled up, and her body wilted.

He caught her before she hit the floor and lifted her in his arms. Her head lolled against his shoulder, and she moaned. His heart clenched. He yanked off the sheets from the nearest table and laid her down. "What's wrong with her? She gave no indication of being ill."

Sister Greene chuckled. "Nothing a bit of sleep won't cure, and if you weren't so enamored with the girl, you'd have pronounced the same diagnosis. She's been awake for thirty hours, maybe more. Before being your girl Friday, she worked a full shift in the motor pool."

"She didn't tell me." He scrubbed at his face with clammy fingers. He'd ignore the nurse's comment about his infatuation. "I didn't know."

"Don't beat yourself up. Many times, staff have worked around the clock. This won't be the first nor the last time she will pull a long day."

He studied Doris's face. "She may also be dehydrated. Please set her up with intravenous fluids. One bag to start. I'll stop by to check on her."

"Yes, sir."

Footsteps faded, and he was alone. He sagged against the table and bowed his head. "Lord, please take care of our girl. Thank you for her steadfast support tonight. I don't deserve her loyalty, not with the way I've treated her. Forgive me, Father, and give her a nudge to forgive me as well."

Ron rubbed at his chest, tight with anxiety. He'd made a fool of himself in front of Sister Greene. Unconscionable. He wouldn't let that happen again.

Chapter Eight

Doris yawned, and her jaw popped. She rubbed her eyes and wandered toward the small pond visible at the edge of the woods. She'd awakened to find herself in one of the hospital beds, blankets tucked to her chin, a gown in place of her soiled uniform. According to Sister Greene, she'd fainted moments after the last surgery was finished then slept around the clock. So much for her stellar career as an OR nurse.

Her face flamed, and she picked up her pace. Fortunately, today was her regularly scheduled day off, so she'd fled the building as soon as one of the junior cadet nurses brought her a change of clothes. She fingered the envelope in her pocket that contained letters from her parents and her sister Cora. The big news in both was her sister Emily's wedding announcement.

She'd found the man of her dreams somewhere in Europe during some sort of hush-hush assignment, and they'd married. Her new husband was American, but because of the nature of her employment, Emily couldn't share more information. Wait until the family heard about Ron being here. They'd traveled over three thousand miles to run into each other.

Sunshine warmed her back as she approached the small body of water. A wooden bench on the berm at the pond's edge invited her to sit and enjoy the view. Cloudless, the sky was robin's-egg blue. The breeze carried a sweet aroma from the field of wildflowers. War seemed nonexistent on a day like this.

Her parent's letter was chatty and contained the local gossip of their tiny town. Scrap drives, bond rallies, and bandage-rolling parties drew the residents together in a common cause. The casualty list was short but depressing nonetheless. Boys who would never grow to be men, and families who would be forever impacted by the loss.

Were Mom and Dad happy they'd been blessed with daughters rather than sons? That their children would never see combat? Granted, they'd lost Cora's husband at Pearl, but the family had only met him a few times. She barely remembered what he looked like. Her grief was more for Cora. Doris and Emily may not bear arms, but their presence in England brought a danger all its own. Did Emily worry about losing her new husband?

She shook her head to dispel the morbid thoughts. Better to think about the blessings. A job she loved and working with people she enjoyed. An education she could never experience in college, and a chance to visit places she might never have seen. In many ways, England looked like home, but the birds she caught sight of during her travels were unfamiliar.

How much longer would the war last? Reports of the Allies' success in Italy excited everyone, and word was that a surrender might occur by late summer. However, Mussolini and his countrymen were only a fraction of the evils, with Hitler remaining the biggest obstacle, although Cora might disagree. Japan killed her husband. How many more Americans would die at the hands of the emperor? Would Cora find another man to love her?

What about herself?

Ron's image invaded her thoughts, and she smiled. Assisting him in surgery had been thrilling and fulfilling. Well, as long as she didn't look at the patient during the procedure. She'd almost lost her lunch with his first incision. Even now, the memory created waves of nausea. She swallowed and raked her fingers through her hair.

Better to think about how kind he'd been when she'd made mistakes while handing him instruments. The man performed intricate, lifesaving procedures, and she was all thumbs. Good thing she worked on cars instead of people. Engine emergencies weren't life threatening.

He hadn't treated her like an equal, but he'd been respectful. And gone above and beyond the call of duty when he carried her to the hospital bed, according to Sister Green. Her face warmed. He must be strong as an ox to lift someone of her height and weight. The nurse also said he'd sat by her bed long into the night.

Was his interest purely professional, or did he feel the same tingles she did when they touched? Why did her heart not realize a relationship was neither possible nor practical? A mechanic and a doctor? A frog and a horse had more in common than she did with Ron.

Ron was a highly educated, skilled physician. She'd barely made it through a year of college, and she tinkered on cars. His misogynistic behaviors had faded for the most part, but he would probably never allow a wife to work outside the home, especially in a garage full of men. He'd want her at home having babies and cooking dinner, waiting for his return with his pipe and slippers. She frowned. Life would be easier if she remained single. God wouldn't saddle some poor guy with the likes of her. The sooner she got used to that idea, the better.

———————◆———————

Hands stuffed into his pockets, Ron sauntered along the gravel path that curved through the estate's property. A slight breeze caressed his sun-warmed cheeks as clouds scudded overhead in the azure sky. Squirrels chattered among the grove of trees that separated the main house from the servants' quarters and outbuildings.

He'd finished his rounds and reports, and the walls of the stately home had become oppressive, so he'd escaped to the outdoors in an effort to clear his head. The opportunity to direct the activities of the hospital seemed exciting at the onset, but the volume of required paperwork put a damper on his enthusiasm. Surgery was his gift, not pushing a pencil, however, the job would look good on his résumé for when the war finally ceased.

Sunlight glinted off the surface of the pond at the edge of the property. He wasn't a fisherman, but perhaps circling the small body of water would give his mind something to do other than fret about patients, staff, and administrative activities. He shaded his eyes with his hand and squinted. Someone sat, head bowed, on the bench near the shore. The individual moved, and he sucked in a breath.

Doris.

His footsteps halted. Should he give her privacy? He surveyed the expansive property. Was there somewhere else he could find solace from the chaos? His gaze swung back to her, and she lifted her hand in greeting. His heart picked up speed. She seemed to want his company. With a smile, he hurried the rest of the way to the idyllic spot.

She rose as he approached, her eyes sparkling, but her appearance tentative. "Is something wrong with one of the vehicles? I can be suited up in short order to get cracking on the problem."

"No." He held up one hand. "There are no problems. I needed a break, and this corner of heaven is my favorite place to hide when I need to get away from responsibilities. I see you have discovered its healing properties as well." He gestured to the bench, and they sat. "Are you feeling better? Your color is good, and there are no shadows beneath your eyes."

"Much better." She laced her fingers together. "Albeit embarrassed that I passed out. I've never been one to faint."

"They were extenuating circumstances. Sister Greene indicated you'd been awake more than thirty hours. A body can only take so much before it must shut down."

A smirk creased her face. "At least I didn't go down during surgery. That would have put a damper on the proceedings."

"Without a doubt." He snickered and stretched out his legs. "Seriously, I do appreciate your help. Two of the nurses are still ill, and two more are showing early symptoms, so we've had to take them out of the rotation."

Doris blanched. "You're not going to ask me to fill in again, are you?"

"I've requested temporary help from London. You should be in the clear."

She swiped her hand across her forehead and grinned. "Whew! Close one."

He looked down his nose in mock sternness. "This time."

"Yeah, I think I've got an engine to maintain somewhere." She cocked her head and blew out a breath. "Did you ever think you'd been halfway around the globe treating patients in a castle?"

"Technically, the estate isn't a castle, but the house is certainly the biggest home I've ever seen. Bigger than even old Mr. Ellis's mansion."

"His house is a monstrosity. I'd forgotten about that place. He would yell at us kids if we made too much noise walking past on the way home from school. At the time, he scared me, but now I wonder if he was lonely or sick. Otherwise, why would he be mean to children?"

"You've got a good heart, Doris. Don't take this as denigrating your current vocation, your compassion would make you a marvelous nurse. Well, except for the possibility of keeling over at the sight of blood."

"Hey, that was only at first. I held my own, thank you very much."

"Yes, you did."

"Thanks. That means a lot coming from you." She giggled, and her cheeks bloomed with color. "To have graduated from Dartmouth and Johns Hopkins, you must be very smart. You've seen lots of nurses during your career."

A stone caught his attention, and he bent to pick it up. Smooth and flat, the pebble was perfect for skipping. He stood and flung the rock, and it bounced three times along the surface of the water. Movement sounded behind him, and he whirled. Doris whipped her arm toward the pond and grinned in satisfaction. He turned back to the pond as her stone hopped four times then disappeared below the surface.

She gave him a saucy smile then danced a jig around the bench.

He raised an eyebrow. "Is everything a competition with you?"

"This coming from the guy who tried to win every award in high school? You're sore because I beat you."

"Okay, best out of three."

"Let me guess, you want to start over."

"That would only be fair."

Doris shrugged and walked to the edge of the pond. She rummaged on the ground until she found three pebbles.

He followed her and found three of his own then bowed and gestured toward the water. "Ladies first."

She curtsied, and with lightning speed heaved a rock that skittered four times then dropped. In rapid succession, she tossed the remaining stones which bounced four and five times respectively.

Heart pounding like he'd run a marathon, he slung the first stone that sunk after two skips. He rolled his eyes and sent the other two rocks sailing. One skipped three times, the other four times. Drat. She'd bested him, but if he were honest, he wasn't disappointed.

"I won, I won, I won." Doris cavorted and pranced along the waterline, her face beaming. She stopped and stood, hands on her hips. "Nice try, Dr. McCann. Weren't you all-American in football? Guess those skills have degenerated with time."

He grabbed her and pretended to throw her into the water.

She screamed and tried to extricate herself from his grip.

Inching toward the pond, his hands still clutched her upper arms. "Let's hope the water is warm, Miss Strealer." He made another fake attempt at tossing her, and his feet skidded on the mud. She slipped from his grasp and landed in the pond with a splash. His arms pinwheeled, and gravity pulled him forward, immersing him over his head.

He popped above the surface. Beside him, she sputtered and wiped moisture from her face. Soaking wet, her hair hung in ropes.

Eyes wide, he waited for her anger to spew forth and held up his hands in surrender. "I am so sorry."

She pushed a wave of water toward him, and her laughter rang out. "You'll pay for this, Ron. Maybe not today, and maybe not tomorrow, but I will get you back."

"I look forward to it, Doris." More than she knew.

Chapter Nine

Doris squinted through the cloud of cigarette smoke that hung over the tables in the pub like morning fog. The cacophony of voices, music from the jukebox, and cutlery on dishes reverberated inside her head. Why she'd agreed to come out after her shift was a mystery. Hours on her feet and hunching over the engine compartment of a particularly ornery ambulance had chewed up most of her day, topped off with a three-hour round trip for supplies.

She sighed and rubbed her forehead to ease the throbbing. Her eyes and throat burned. Next time she would provide a politely worded excuse then curl up on her bed with a book and a cup of tea.

Maureen poked her. "What'll you have, Doris? Beer or wine?"

"Neither." She smiled at the waitress. "Just tea and a glass of water for me."

"Right away, luv." The woman poked the pencil into her bun and sashayed between the tables to the bar.

"Are you going to be a wet blanket, Doris?"

"Nope, just not interested in alcohol, Maureen. I'm groggy enough after the hours I put in today. Aren't you?"

Maureen shrugged. "I need something to unwind, and beer is just the ticket." She cast her gaze from one side of the room to the other. "Then I'm going to find me a healthy man with two feet who can dance the night away. You should try it."

"I'm torn. Ages have passed since the last time I danced, but my dogs are killing me."

"With the right man, you'll forget about the pain." Maureen laughed. "But the ache will be worth it in the end."

The waitress returned with their drinks, and Doris lifted the water to her lips. Cool liquid soothed her parched throat, and she drank half before putting down the glass. A split second of silence then the jukebox belted out Glenn Miller's "Jukebox Saturday Night." Cheers filled the room, and couples ran to the dance floor.

"I love this song." Maureen jumped up. "Wanna join me?"

"Maybe in a bit. I'd like to drink my tea while it's hot."

"Suit yourself, but you're not going to find a partner while stuck here in the corner."

Doris picked up the cup and wrapped her hands around its warmth. "Later."

Arms waving and hips swaying, Maureen performed the samba as she merged into the undulating crowd.

Time passed, and the Andrews Sisters' voices warbled "Boogie Woogie Bugle Boy" from the machine, then Judy Garland serenaded the dancers with "Zing! Went the Strings of My Heart." Doris tapped her foot and hummed along with the music. Maureen danced past the table in the arms of a navy officer who seemed smitten with her friend. Several other girls from the hospital mingled with soldiers, sailors, and locals who laughed and gyrated to the tunes.

A short, broad-shouldered sergeant paused in front of her. He bowed deeply from the waist, his arm outstretched. "May I have this dance, miss?"

She glanced from him to the joyous expressions of the couples and then back to his eager face. The GI seemed harmless enough and deserved some fun. She shrugged and clasped his fingers. He pulled her to her feet then drew her close but not too close. His hand rested lightly on her waist, and he whirled her along the edge of the dance floor. He was no Gene Kelly, but his moves were smooth and sure. She relaxed in his embrace as he made small talk.

The music pulsed, and Doris reveled in its beat. Maureen was right. Despite her tired feet, she enjoyed dancing with a nice man. A few minutes later, the song was over, and the slow strains of "The White Cliffs of Dover" seeped from the jukebox. She remained in the sergeant's arms for a few measures, then a naval officer tapped him on the shoulder cutting in. He released her with a smile, and her new partner grasped her hand and placed his hand on her waist.

He was not nearly as skilled as the sergeant, but he had yet to tread on her toes as many of the girls complained about on Sunday mornings after a night at the pub. Mute, he looked everywhere except at her. His damp palm clung to her dry one, and she smiled to herself. As nervous as he seemed to be, how had he worked up the courage to ask her to dance? The music ended, and he let go of her hand as if burned. A quick bow, then he disappeared into the sea of people.

She blinked at his retreating figure. Weird. Feeling awkward as a lone woman in the crowd, she threaded through the tables toward the door. Time to leave.

Before she could reach the exit, a lanky man with dark hair and wearing an army dress uniform grabbed her hand and twirled her toward the crowd. His sloppy grin and unfocused eyes spoke of the number of drinks he'd imbibed. She tried to extricate her fingers, but he maintained his firm grasp. "Excuse me, sir, I must be on my way."

"No way, sister, things are just getting good. You need to stay and keep me company. I outrank you, see?" He pointed to the bars on his shoulder then yanked her toward him in a crushing embrace. "Dancing with Lieutenant Halifax will be the most fun you'll have tonight."

Trapped in his arms and pressed against chest, she couldn't catch her breath. "Please let me go, sir. I'm tired and would like to go home."

His face brightened. "You're inviting me to your place? Fabulous." A wolfish gleam sparkled in his eyes. "We can get to know each other even better."

"No, that's not what I mean." She struggled to extricate herself, but his grip tightened, and she tried not to panic. Surely, the man wouldn't try anything inappropriate in a room full of people. Who was she kidding?

His behavior was already improper, and he seemed intent upon dragging her outside. *Lord, save me.*

———————————◆———————————

Ron sauntered toward the pub with two of the other hospital physicians. He'd allowed them to talk him into an evening out. Bereft of excuses, he acquiesced when the men threatened to hogtie him and carry his carcass into town. A quick cola and some socializing with the guys, and he could call it a night. He might not be much of a dancer, but it would be fun to hear the latest tunes from all the big singers.

Rumor had it that Dinah Shore planned to bring her backup band to the hospital and do a set for the injured men, and that she might stop by the pub for a few numbers. He doubted a classy actress like Miss Shore would darken the door of the local bar, but if he were wrong, he'd try to get close enough to meet her.

"Look at me. I'm Fred Astaire." Dr. Frankel executed a series of tap-dancing steps, then broke into a foxtrot with an invisible partner. "Bet none of you chaps can do that."

"You win, Frankel. You're the best hoofer we've got." Ron shrugged. "Try not to show up the ladies with those moves."

"He won't, but I might." Dr. Yaskinsky performed the rumba, an exaggerated look of seriousness on his face. "I'm gonna knock those gals' socks off."

"I didn't realize I was in the presence of greatness, gentlemen. I'm impressed. Since I can't possibly do any better, I won't embarrass you by making any attempts."

"Surely you're not that bad, McCann. We'll find some pretty gal who doesn't mind a lesser man."

"Hey, I may not dance as well as you two knuckleheads, but I'm definitely not the lesser man." Ron shook his head. These guys' egos knew no bounds. "There are plenty of ladies who would want to keep a great catch like me company.

"Now you're looking for a wife?" Dr. Yaskinsky widened his eyes in mock surprise. "The unapproachable Dr. McCann wants to settle down? I'm shocked and amazed."

"Laugh it up, Yaskinsky."

"I plan to."

They arrived at the pub. Music and voices filtered outside from behind the closed door. Ron frowned. With the noise level loud enough to be heard from here, he was going to shatter an eardrum.

"Listen, guys—"

"Oh, no you don't." Frankel yanked open the door, and Yaskinsky grabbed his arms and propelled Ron into the dim, pulsating pub. "Let the games begin."

With his arms still pinned to his sides by Yaskinsky, Ron surveyed the room through the smoky haze. A handful of couples danced in the center of the room. Conversation buzzed above the music. The smell of garlic, onions, and fried fish permeated the air. "We'll never find a vacant booth in this crowd."

Frankel grinned. "Then we'll have to crash someone's party." He jerked his head toward a nearby table at which three young women chattered. "One for each of us. Perfect."

"But—"

"Come on. Are you going to be a wet blanket the whole time?" They pushed through the throng to the trio of girls where Frankel puffed out his chest. "Hello, ladies. Are these seats taken?"

As one, the gals giggled and shook their heads. Ron rolled his eyes. No Mensa candidates here. He forced a smile and dropped into the chair farthest from the women. The doctors sat on either side of the women, and Frankel gestured to a waitress. "Oi! We're ready to order."

Ron pressed his lips together. The men were highly regarded, serious-minded professionals at the hospital, and their arrival at the bar had turned them into boorish simpletons.

The waitress came to the table, her expression harried and fatigued. "What can I get you?"

"Ladies first." Frankel motioned at the girls.

At least, the men hadn't lost all their manners. While he waited for his tablemates to order, he looked around the room. Soldiers, sailors, and airmen mingled with men in civvies. Off duty or locals? Women in a rainbow of dresses brightened the dim interior. He recognized several of the employees and volunteers from the hospital. They worked hard, so it was nice to see them get away and relax. Why did he find it so difficult to do the same?

Movement near the bar caught his attention, and he squinted through the murky air. Was the woman in the dazzling blue dress Doris Strealer?

"Ron?"

He turned his attention to the table where the waitress stood, pencil poised over a notepad.

"Er…sorry…I'll have a Moxie."

"He'll have a beer," Yaskinsky shouted.

"No, just the cola for me." He narrowed his eyes at the man. "One of us should have a clear head tomorrow."

The doctors guffawed, and Ron gave the serving girl an apologetic smile. She scribbled on the page then hurried toward the kitchen.

Ron glanced over his shoulder at the woman in blue. Back to him, the tall, slender, and graceful figure with flowing brown hair towered over her date who stood entirely too close to her with a hand on her shoulder.

"Seems someone has caught your eye, McCann. Too bad she appears to be taken." Frankel gestured to the women at the table. "Don't be rude. We've got company right here."

"Sorry, chaps. I thought I recognized one of the motor corps drivers. She looks a bit different not wearing her coveralls." Ron tugged at his collar. Very different.

Their drinks arrived, and Ron drank his soda like a dying man trapped in the desert. Anything to shift the focus away from him. Fortunately, the doctors seemed so intent on impressing the ladies at the table, they ignored him.

He shifted his chair and peered at the woman across the room. She turned. It was Doris. In her uniform, she was beautiful. In evening attire, she was breathtaking. What did she see in the scrawny man who sported lieutenant's bars and leered at her like a piranha ready to strike? She hadn't struck him as a girl who liked that sort of thing.

"Let's dance." Dr. Frankel rose and held out his arm to the blonde he'd been seated next to. They skirted the table, and he leaned close to Ron. "You've been bitten by the love bug, *Doctor.* You might want to get a prescription for that."

"What—"

The couple brushed past and made their way to the dance floor.

Love bug. Not hardly. Ron took another swig from his drink. Granted, Doris was gorgeous and intelligent, but they had nothing in common and both had a job to do. Relationships during war were not a good idea. Either one of them could be transferred…or worse. Their near misses with the air raid were proof of the uncertainly of life in a war zone. No, he could appreciate her smarts and good looks, but admiration from afar would be the extent of his involvement.

Chapter Ten

Glenn Miller's "I've Got a Gal in Kalamazoo" burst from the jukebox. Men and women paired off and rushed to the center of the room to dance. The wooden floor vibrated in rhythm with their steps, and Ron drummed his fingers on the table in time with the music. His favorite bandleader, Miller, had forsaken his career to join the military last autumn to his fans' dismay. The navy rejected him, but the army had welcomed him with open arms. His last concert in September as a civilian had been a sellout.

The crowd of gyrating couples blocked his view of Doris. Probably a good thing. With any luck, not watching her with another man would remove her from his mind. He forced a smile and looked at the young women across the table. "Are you ladies having a good time? I'm not much of a dancer, but I'd be willing to give it a go."

Louise, dressed in a pale yellow dress with her hair done in victory rolls, shook her head. "I've got two left feet that have done a lot of walking in the wards today. I'm happy listening to the tunes." She looked at her tablemate. "Rhoda loves to dance. She can show you how it's done."

Wearing a crimson dress and ill-fitting black sweater, Rhoda gave Ron a tentative smile. Plain with shoulder-length brown hair and nondescript brown eyes, she probably didn't get many offers. Unfair, but true in an environment where every day could be someone's last, and having a good time was paramount.

He rose and held out his hand. "May I have this dance?"

A startled look crossed the young woman's face, then her expression bloomed in gratitude transforming her appearance. "Yes, thank you, Dr. McCann." She grasped his fingers, and they made their way to the dance floor as the song switched to "Be Careful, It's My Heart."

Ron pulled her into his arms, and her floral perfume enveloped him. "With the slower song, you won't have to worry about me trouncing your toes too often."

"After my first visit to the pub, I learned to wear closed-toe pumps. The injuries aren't quite as bad." She giggled, and her cheeks reddened. "And I am a nurse, so I can perform my own first aid."

He chuckled. "You're a good egg. Do you come here often?" He cringed. Not exactly a smooth operator, but he tried to keep the clichéd lines to a minimum. "Well…"

"Once or twice a week after shift. I don't drink, but the opportunity to hear music sometimes helps me to forget the war and the boys I take care of."

"I've seen injuries I never imagined possible." He released her waist a*nd twirled her.

"You're a better dancer than you think." Her eyes lit, then she sobered up. "None of us will never be the same, but hopefully the experience will make me more compassionate, a better nurse."

"Commendable."

They danced in silence, and Ron concentrated on not stepping on Rhoda's feet. Periodically jostled by another couple, he tightened his grip on her hand. "Don't want to lose you in the crowd."

"You're very gallant, Doctor." She tilted her head. "I hope you won't mind me saying this, but you're nothing like the nurses say."

"Hard-nosed and difficult?"

"Not those words, but...I'm sorry, I've insulted you. That wasn't my intention. I'm trying to tell you how much I'm enjoying myself, and I'm bungling it."

"No need to apologize. Your colleagues are correct. My overbearing nature has been recently brought to my attention." Doris's face flashed across his mind, and his chest tightened. She'd made no bones about his arrogance, but their recent encounter at the lake when they'd been dunked seemed to soften her attitude toward him.

The music ended, and Rhoda applauded. "Thank you, Doctor. You did well. I'm unscathed." She squeezed his arm. "And now, I must head to the barracks to grab some shut-eye. Early shift."

"Would you like an escort? The hour is late."

She waved a hand in dismissal. "I'll be fine, but thanks for the offer."

"Thank you for the dance…and for your candor. I look forward to seeing you in the future." He cleared his throat. Would she think he was indicating a romantic interest? What had he done? "I…uh…"

Her eyes widened, and she patted his arm. "That's kind of you, Doctor, but I have a beau. He's with the Fifth Army somewhere in Italy if I read his letters correctly."

His face warmed. She thought he wanted a relationship and was letting him down gently. He swallowed a laugh at the irony of the situation. In the past, it had always been him walking away from any entanglements. The tables were turned. Doris would relish that tidbit of information. "You must miss him terribly."

A shadow darkened her face for a brief moment. "I do."

"You can count on me as a friend, Rhoda. Nothing more. I'd be honored to be your dance partner should you want a turn around the floor occasionally to forget this raging conflict."

"I'd like that, Doctor." She smoothed her skirts and melted into the crowd.

Bemused, he watched her go. Doris would like the woman, and she'd love knowing Rhoda had told him about his reputation for being difficult.

Was Doris still here?

"I said, I'm not interested. Please leave me alone."

Ron whirled. If he wasn't mistaken, the warm alto voice belonged to Doris. He scanned the room, his eyes searching for the beautiful brunette in the deep-blue dress. There. At the end of the bar, the same squirt who'd been so close to her earlier, held her with one hand and stroked her cheek with the other. Even in the dimness, her face looked pale, and fear darkened her eyes.

"You know you want me, baby. Stop struggling. I'll show you a good time."

Doris twisted her neck. "If you were last man on the planet, I wouldn't want you. Unhand me, or you'll be sorry."

Muscles quivering, Ron clenched his fists and strode toward her. She may not want his interference, but it appeared the loser wasn't going to take no for an answer.

The man pushed his face close to Doris's. "And how do you plan to do that?"

In a flash, she pulled back her leg and kicked him in the shin.

Howling, he hopped on one foot and rubbed his injured limb. "How dare you." He drew back his arm as if to hit her, and Ron grabbed his arm.

"That's enough. She is not interested in your presence, and neither are the rest of us." Ron spoke through gritted teeth. "If you know what's good for you, you'll get out before I finish what the lady started."

"This isn't over. A girl's reputation is easily sullied in this small town. She'll wish she hadn't done what she did."

Ron caught the man's lapels between his fists and shoved him against the counter. "I suggest you rethink that strategy. Show some respect to the lady and the uniform you're wearing. Now, crawl back down the hole you came from, and don't show yourself here ever again. Clear?"

His antagonist's bravado faltered, and he struggled to extricate himself from Ron's grip. "She didn't tell me she had a boyfriend." He turned toward Doris. "I beg your pardon, miss. Won't never happen again," he whined. With a hard tug, he yanked his jacket out of Ron's hands and scurried toward the door.

Doris wilted, and Ron wrapped his arm around her shoulder before she could fall. "Are you all right? I would have come over sooner had I known his attentions were unwanted."

She closed her eyes and blew out a deep breath. "I thought I could control him...you know, my height...but he kept pawing at me." Her lips trembled. "Thank you for saving me. I'm not sure what would have happened if you hadn't come along."

"Don't cry. Your kick was a good start."

Tears glistened in her eyes. "Nice of you to say, but I feel much safer knowing you're around."

Ron's chest swelled. He could get used to protecting her.

Chapter Eleven

The cement floor chilled Doris's back through her coveralls as she lay underneath the first of three ambulances she needed to tune-up before the end of the day. Finished with changing the oil, she scanned the condition of the axle, tie rods, and the oil pan. Despite the vehicle's age, there was little rust evident on the undercarriage.

She smiled in satisfaction and brushed an errant strand of hair out of her eyes. Creating a regular maintenance schedule for the cars, trucks, and ambulances gave the staff regular work, and prevented breakdowns like the one Ron had experienced a few weeks ago.

Her smile dimmed. He'd been so gracious walking her to the barracks after the altercation with the lieutenant. She shuddered and scooted out from under the vehicle then climbed to her feet. What would have happened had Ron not come along when he did? Ticking off the completed tasks, she ran her finger along the list.

The fuel pump system was next. Good. Hopefully, the tedium of disassembling and cleaning the part would keep her from dwelling on last night's debacle. Her roommate had scoffed at Doris's concerns the guy would make trouble, and she'd even intimated that Doris had brought the problem on herself by looking so pretty.

Was the girl right? Would making herself unattractive prevent being manhandled? She frowned. Just because there weren't lots of girls around, the men shouldn't be allowed to treat women poorly.

Doris marked the fuel pump cover and body position before removing the pump from the engine compartment. Fortunately, with this ambulance model she wouldn't be required to empty the fuel tank to take care of the part. She rotated the pump to check for gummed, damaged, or tilted valves. So far, so good.

Too bad life wasn't as easy as maintaining a car. Why were men so confusing? First, Ron was beastly, a caveman with his out-of-date beliefs about women and their place. Then he changed his tune and began to treat her like the professional she was. Her face warmed. She knew better than to attribute his playfulness at the pond to flirting, but she'd caught him staring at her twice since then. What was he thinking when he looked at her? He was not the guy she used to know in high school, but if she were honest with herself, she was no longer the same girl.

She blew out the valve chamber and checked for particles that would prevent the part from seating correctly. Scrounging around on the table, she found the oil she needed to coat the connection. The tiny drops lubricated the metal, and she reassembled the valves. Why couldn't relationships between men and women be smoothed as simply as car parts.

The lieutenant who'd accosted her last night threatened to ruin her reputation. He was part of the military. Would she be sent home in disgrace? Ron assured her the guy was too loaded to remember his accusations, and the whole incident would blow over without a whimper. Why couldn't she believe him?

A yawn overtook her. She'd lain awake most of the night wondering if she should report the episode to the motor corps supervisor or if disclosing the episode would make the situation worse.

With practiced motions, she reassembled the valves and turned her attention to the diaphragms. A quick inspection told her they were still in good condition, without scuffs or torn spots. She pulled a tin can half filled with kerosene toward her and dropped the diaphragms into the liquid to soak.

Mom would remind her to soak her problems with prayer. She should have thought of that sooner instead of worrying herself into sleeplessness.

She heaved a sigh and pulled a rag from her back pocket then wiped her hands. Bowing her head, she closed her eyes. "Dear Father God, please forgive my unbelief. I constantly run ahead of You and fail to listen to Your still, small voice. I fret about my circumstances, even those I can't control. Thank You for Ron and his willingness to get involved to help me out of the situation. If there are consequences from the incident at the bar, please help me face them with grace. Help me to walk the path You have set for me and to stop getting ahead of myself…and You. Amen."

Warmth engulfed her, and the tightness in her chest eased. "Thank You for Your peace, Lord."

Opening her eyes, she hummed her favorite hymn. The day no longer hung heavy on her shoulders.

———————•—•———————

Ron stepped out of the car and slammed the door. After a night of tossing and turning, he'd decided that a visit to the military regional liaison would kill two birds, as the saying went. The man needed to know about the incident with Doris in case it blew up in their faces. Blindsiding the higher-ups was never a good idea, so rather than simply submit a communique that might get mislaid, he would make the report in person. He would also ask for military police to prevent future issues.

He paused at the bottom of the stairs and admired the sandstone mansion, another country home owned by a member of the peerage and requisitioned by the British government. In America, the house would be called a castle. Soaring towers flanked the entryway, and there were a dozen windows on the three floors of each wing. The intricate landscaping surrounding the building was tired looking, obviously no longer kept by groundsmen. What would it be like to have enough income to purchase and maintain multiple mammoth houses?

A slight breeze rippled the leaves of the large shrubs with white flowers, their sweet scent swirling around him. Border plants bobbed their blossoms from the edge of the once-manicured garden. He turned and surveyed the grassy expanse. Trees, hedges, and raised beds dotted the hills. Picturesque and soothing.

The front door opened with a bang, and he pivoted on his heel. A pair of lieutenants emerged and slapped their visored caps on their heads then trotted down the stairs. Engaged in heated debate, they barely acknowledged his presence. Arrogant pups. He blinked. Did he used to resemble them in his climb to the top?

Enough. Ron scrubbed at his face, then smoothed his suit and climbed the stairs. He pulled open the door and entered the foyer. Lined with windows, the massive entryway was bright with sunlight. Gilt-framed portraits stared at him from either side of the room. Nestled in the corner, a young woman sat behind a large, wooden desk.

She smiled as he approached. "May I help you, sir?"

Wearing the khaki-colored uniform of the Women's Army Corps, her blonde hair was pulled back in a severe bun at the base of her head. Round, gold-rimmed spectacles accentuated her blue eyes. She couldn't be more than twenty years old. Was the military so desperate to take girls barely out of high school?

"I have an appointment with Major General Isaacson."

"He's expecting you." She motioned to the marble staircase. "Up those stairs, then left. His office is the fourth door on the right."

"Thank you." Ron hurried up the steps, his hand on the gleaming wooden rail. How many servants did the gentry require to ensure every nook and cranny was sparkling? He arrived in front of the door and straightened his spine. This was worse than appearing before the medical board.

He rapped once on the doorframe, and a deep voice barked from inside, "Come in!" Heart in his throat, Ron entered the opulent suite. Flocked wallpaper covered with more gilt-framed portraits greeted him. A stone fireplace graced one wall, and the rug under his feet was Persian, no doubt. Most of the furniture seemed to harken from a bygone era.

Isaacson rose and gestured to a cluster of upholstered chairs near the window. The only comfortable looking seats in the room.

"Thank you, sir." Ron sank into the chair. The drive from the hospital over rutted roads had been arduous, and the cushions enveloped him like a glove. "And thank you for seeing me. You're a busy man, so I'll be quick. I'm the director at Heritage Hall Hospital in Hemel Hempstead, and we had an incident at one of the nearby pubs involving one of the soldiers from the Ninth Air Force and one of the Red Cross girls. I wanted you to be aware of it and to discuss what sort of discipline should be meted out as a result."

The major general raised his left eyebrow. "Sounds serious."

With minimal words, Ron recounted the episode with Doris and the drunken lieutenant. "Such behavior must violate the code, sir, don't you think?"

"The men are a long way from home, Dr. McCann, many of them for the first time. Homesickness combined with fear and boredom sometimes brings out the worst in these boys. Add liquor, well…" He shrugged. "We need to give the chaps some leeway. Besides, who's to say the young lady didn't encourage the guy?"

Ron bolted upright. "Encourage…no sir…I know the girl in question, and she was definitely not looking to be…ah…intimate with the man. He took unwanted liberties, and she should expect justice."

"Then why didn't she accompany you or make a formal complaint?"

"She doesn't know I'm here."

Major General Isaacson studied him for a long moment, and Ron schooled his features to remain impassive. Finally, when the silence had thickened to the consistency of heavy fog, Isaacson crossed his arms and stared at the vacant fireplace. "Look, I'm sure this lieutenant's behavior was a disgrace, but no one got hurt, and the girl got off unscathed, right? If I transferred or tossed every soldier who stepped out of line into the stockade, we'd be shorthanded to fight that villain, Hitler."

"But—"

"Don't interrupt."

Ron's face heated. Junior move. "Yes, sir."

"Give me the man's name, and I'll ensure he's reprimanded, but your job is to manage the hospital not get involved in military affairs. Butt out, and leave the situation alone. If you know this girl as well as you say, use your influence to encourage her to forget about the whole episode. These young women are out of their element coming over here, mingling with the troops. They're too sensitive and bound to get offended. She should give the issue a rest and go about her job. That's why she's here. Understood?"

Did he have any choice? Ron rose. "Yes, sir." The odds of the man agreeing to a military police presence were slim. "I'll see myself out."

"Good. And McCann, don't risk your career by being a hero where you don't belong."

Chapter Twelve

Heart pounding, Doris dashed into the barracks and changed out of her coveralls. Fortunately, she hadn't started work on the vehicles, so there was no need to scrub grease from under her fingernails. She grabbed her purse then stopped in front of the mirror one of the gals had hung near the door. A quick inspection of her image in the glass made her frown. Her hair was drawn into a haphazard ponytail, and she'd foregone any makeup. Normally not a problem, her appearance needed to change now that Ron was going to tag along.

In an effort to save on gas, or petrol as the Brits liked to say, Sister Greene indicated that Doris would drop off Ron for his meeting then pick up the supplies before circling back to retrieve the good doctor. A full day, when she'd only planned to be gone until lunchtime.

She rummaged in her handbag and found her comb. With a quick tug, she pulled off the band from her hair and detangled the mess. More digging in her pocketbook unearthed her cosmetics, and she sponged rouge across her cheeks and applied light-pink lipstick.

Behind her, the clock struck the hour, so she stuffed her belongings back into her bag. She tilted her head then leaned closer to the reflection. Her height was bad enough. Why did her hair have to be such a nondescript shade of brown and her eyes set so close together? She shrugged. Their journey was an errand, not a date. What did it matter how she looked?

One last glance at herself, and she hurried from the barracks, slamming the door. Making her way to the garage, she signed out one of the four-ton cargo trucks and grabbed the keys. She checked the fuel level, scrutinized the tires, and tugged at the rope knots to ensure the canvas cover would remain in place. Not the most comfortable of the fleet, but today's trip was about supplies, not passengers.

Doris hoisted herself into the vehicle, started the engine, and rumbled out of the garage. She guided the unwieldy truck along the gravel lane and stopped in front of the hospital, resisting the urge to check her image in the side mirror. An errand, not a date.

She wet her dry lips and drummed her fingers on the steering wheel. Should she go inside to notify Ron that daylight was burning? Wasn't he on a schedule? Sunshine warmed her through the windshield, promising a hot day of driving. She'd take a cloudless scorcher over the darkness or a drenching rain any time.

The enormous door opened at the top of the stairs, and Ron emerged, his black doctor's satchel gripped in his right hand, and a newspaper tucked under the arm. He squinted in her direction then waved as he trotted down the steps. Sunlight burnished his sandy-blonde hair, and his face shone. Broad shoulders strained against his suit jacket, and his slacks hung from his narrow waist. Doris pressed her hand against her middle where a dray of squirrels seemed to have taken up residence. Ron had transformed from the awkward, gangly teen into an Adonis, and she was done for if she couldn't get her erratic pulse to take a holiday.

He tossed his bag on the floor of the passenger seat before heaving himself onto the seat beside her. "A delightful day for a drive. Thanks for going out of your way to drop me off. I'm sure my little side trip put a kink in your plans."

"Not too badly." She put the truck in motion and swallowed a sigh. Why had she never noticed the dimple in his left cheek? "Unfortunately, you're in for a rough ride in this baby."

"I'll try not to fall out." He chuckled and pretended to cling to the armrest.

She forced herself not to stare his sparkling hazel eyes that crinkled at the edges when he smiled. Rough didn't begin to describe the trip.

They followed the lane through the gate then turned onto the main road, the truck trundling across the deep ridges in the road, the result of too many heavy vehicles traversing the macadam too many times. How long would it take England to regain her beauty after the war?

Ron opened the newspaper and pulled a pencil from the inside pocket of his jacket. "You're in luck. I've gotten hooked on crossword puzzles, and Dr. Muldoon just received a whole stack of the *New York Times* from his wife. He shared them with the staff."

"Nice of him, but I'm not sure how helpful I'll be."

"You're a smart gal." The paper crackled in his hands as he folded the sheet into quarters. "First clue: seven-letter word for fortified line held by Germans."

"Maginot."

"Well done. Okay, next clue which is also a seven-letter word: West African coastal district. Hmmm. That's a tough one."

"Yeah, I'm going to have to pass on that." She grinned. One for two. Not bad. "Move on."

"That's the spirit." He cleared his throat. "Seven letters again. Vast Russian plains."

"Easy one. Steppes."

"Look at you. Already a pro." He waved the paper at her, the tangy scent of his Bay Rum aftershave drifting toward her.

Her toes curled, and her foot slipped off the accelerator. The truck lurched. "Sorry." Face hot, she rolled her eyes. "Guess I should pay closer attention to the road."

"We can just talk if that's better for you." He slid the newspaper beside his satchel on the floor.

She pressed her lips together. So much for impressing him with her knowledge. He must think her a total fathead. "Sure. You talk. I'll drive."

"I can read aloud from the newspaper, if you'd like."

"No, too depressing. We're living the war. We don't need to read about it from some reporter."

"Good point. Too bad Mrs. Muldoon didn't send the sports section."

"You can put in a request for the next batch, which by the time you get them, will be covering football season."

"Perfect."

She glanced over and swallowed. He stared at her, an unreadable expression on his face. Probably trying to figure out why he'd gotten stuck with her again. "Guess the war has impacted the game. Are there enough men to play?"

"Yes, but barely. Between enlistments and the draft, most of the teams have been depleted. There's a rumor that some of the teams will combine which will prove interesting."

"If that happens, picking a favorite will be difficult."

"You've been gracious to discuss sports, but I'm sure you'd rather talk about something else."

"What else do you know besides football and medicine?"

Ron tipped back his head and laughed. "Am I that two-dimensional to you?" He snickered and wiped his eyes. "I'm a regular Renaissance man and can cover any number of topics."

Her breathing hitched. "No...I...well." She giggled and slapped his arm. "Not the caveman as I originally thought when I ran into you at the hospital?"

He fisted his hands and pretended to scratch his sides while grunting. "Absolutely not."

They laughed in unison, and Doris squeezed the steering wheel. Her intentions to stay unencumbered went out the window in his presence. Time to change the subject. "Can you tell me why you're headed to London or is it a secret mission?"

His eyes shuttered, and he crossed his arms. "No secrets. Just boring meetings."

She was no psychologist, but if body language was any indication, he was lying through his teeth.

Chapter Thirteen

Two hours later, Ron was in the cargo truck staring out the passenger side window. He rubbed his forehead as the vehicle did its usual bucking-bronco routine over the uneven roads. Heavy silence permeated the cab. Doris was morose and had barely glanced at him since they'd set out to return to the hospital. One step forward, two steps backward with her. With such moodiness, how had she passed muster with the Red Cross?

Meeting with the regional director had gone as planned including the discussion about changing Ron's assignment—the main reason for his hurried trip this morning. After the man had phoned with the news, Ron urged him to hold off on his decision until they could confer in person. He'd hoped to talk the man out of the possibility but needing a physician skilled in thoracic surgery at one of the London facilities, the director wanted to move him as soon as possible.

Granted, Ron found the administrative tasks tiresome, but the team of doctors, nurses, and orderlies were functioning as a well-oiled engine. He swallowed a laugh. Before spending time with Doris, he never would have understood exactly what the idiom meant. And he was fooling himself if he didn't admit to enjoying their friendship more than he should. So much for remaining aloof.

A bang reverberated throughout the cab then the sound of whooshing as the truck lurched to the right. The vehicle slowed, and flapping vibrated the floor beneath his feet.

Doris blew out a loud breath and guided them off the road. "Flat tire. This is my fault. I didn't inspect them before we set off this morning."

"Maybe we hit something in the road."

"Possibly. Anyway, I'll get it changed as quickly as I can."

"Please let me help."

She glanced over, her eyebrows drawn together. "Aren't you afraid of injuring your hands? A surgeon who can't operate is no good."

"You can handle the dangerous part of the process." He grinned. "But if I stand around and do nothing, my caveman reputation will remain intact."

Her lips quirked, and she nodded. "Fine, but if you get hurt, I won't be held responsible."

He swung down from the truck and trotted to the driver's side.

Doris was already out of the vehicle kneeling over an open metal box on the ground. Tools clanking, she dug around then held up some sort of wrench with a flourish. "There you are!" She crawled between the cab and the truck bed where the spare was stowed. Grunting and mumbling, she wrestled with the bolts that held the tire in place.

Ron hesitated. Should he repeat his offer to help or wait to be told what to do? His father had made it clear that Ron's mechanical skills were sorely lacking. His bumbling efforts might only make the situation worse.

"Stand aside. I'm going to toss down this beast." Doris's voice was muffled as she called out from behind the tire. "On three. One…two…three!" The rubber donut rolled off the truck and hit the earth with a thud, sending a shower of dust airborne. She jumped down and brushed off her hands, a smile of satisfaction lighting her face. A smudge of dirt graced one cheek.

He stifled the urge to rub the spot clean.

She loosened the nuts on the damaged tire, then retrieved the jack and positioned it under the vehicle's frame. She cranked the handle until the tire was off the ground

Hands in his pockets, he sighed. He was as useful as an operating room without a scalpel. "Surely, there's something I can do."

With a glance over her shoulder, she shook her head. "Changing a tire is a one-person job. I'll let you get the next one."

"No, you won't, but I appreciate you saying that."

With agile motions, Doris removed the nuts, slid off the bad tire, and settled the spare in place. "You can hand me the fasteners."

He scrambled forward and picked up the metal orbs. Dropping them into her palm one at a time, he rolled his eyes at the sense of satisfaction that swelled his chest from this small task.

Job finished, she tossed the wrench at the toolbox where it landed with a clatter. She tried to stand and stumbled. He rushed forward to catch her, his arms wrapping around her middle. For a brief moment he maintained his balance before stumbling, and they landed in a heap.

Sprawled on top of him, she blushed, her face a hairsbreadth away from his. He reached up and wiped away the smear of dirt he'd seen earlier. Her pupils dilated, causing her deep-brown eyes to turn inky. A tiny gasp squeaked, and the color on her cheeks deepened. His gaze moved to her lips, soft-looking and inviting. He shifted underneath her, and she jumped up, scuttling away.

Ron blew out a deep breath and sat up. Raking his fingers through his hair, he shook his head while his heartbeat stuttered in his chest. He glanced at Doris bent over the tool chest. The fall had loosened her hair, and a lock hung across her face, hiding her expression. Her hunched shoulders and stiff back told him that she was mortified. He needed to repair the damage.

"I'm sorry for being such an oaf." He stood and retrieved the damaged tire. Rolling it toward the truck, he chuckled. "My caveman image is intact. No self-respecting gentleman drops his lady."

"Not your fault." She tucked the hair behind her ear and glanced at him, her expression a mixture of embarrassment and shame. "If I wasn't so tall, you'd have been able to stay upright."

"Nonsense. I've got eight inches on you. Apparently, my strength isn't what it should be." He flexed his arm and poked at his bicep. "See, not much there." He let out an exaggerated grunt as he hefted the damaged tire onto the back of the cab.

She giggled, and her face lightened. "Let's finish this and get back on the road. I appreciate you trying to make me feel better."

He reached out and stroked her cheek. "I'm not just being kind. You are a beautiful woman, Doris, lithe and graceful, but more importantly, you are beautiful from the inside with a generous heart and steadfast faith. Don't let anyone tell you anything different, even yourself."

Before he could give in to the urge to draw her into a comforting embrace, he boosted himself onto the truck and attached the shredded tire to its rack. He double-checked the tightness of the nuts then lowered himself to the ground.

Doris grabbed the handle of the toolbox, her searching gaze filled with uncertainty and something else. Was it hope?

The day had taken a serious turn. Not what he planned.

He opened the driver's door and bowed. "Your chariot awaits. Let us make haste." He laced his fingers and cupped his hands. "A foothold, m'lady."

She wrinkled her nose then shrugged. Using his hands as a step, she climbed into the vehicle and started the engine. He hurried around the front of the truck and got inside.

"You put any mechanic I've ever known to shame." He rolled down the window to bring a breeze into the stifling hot cab.

"Anyone can change a tire, Ron." A muscle in her jaw jumped. "But the flat shouldn't have happened. I take pride in the procedures I put in place, and I failed to follow them."

"Mistakes happen. The good news is we had a spare, and you were able to replace the bad tire." He sighed. "Who will take care of me in London?"

"What?" Doris's head whipped toward him, her eyes wide.

"I…uh…well…it's not definite yet, but the regional director would like to relocate me to London. Apparently, they're in need of a surgeon with my skills. He has to determine how to replace me here before the decision becomes final."

"When were you going to tell me?" She frowned then waved her hand. "I was foolish to think we had become friends, and you would confide in me."

"We are friends. I was instructed not to say anything." Ron squirmed in the seat. "You have no right to get angry because of something out of my control. Some information is not meant for you women. You girls should focus on doing the jobs you've been tasked with and leave the heavy lifting to the men."

Her eyebrows shot up. "Never mind. You don't owe me or any of the *girls* an explanation." She gripped the steering wheel, her lips set in a thin slash.

"Wait. That came out wrong. There are hierarchies—"

"I don't want to hear anything you have to say."

He clenched his hands and sighed. In the blink of an eye, he'd bungled things again.

Chapter Fourteen

Airplanes buzzed overhead, and sweat broke out on Doris's face. She squinted at the blue expanse above as she guided the ambulance along the remote stretch of highway on the way to the hospital. Would the dark profile of an aircraft always give her the shakes, even after the war?

Tasked with picking up two patients who needed Ron's expertise, she had pushed the vehicle to its limits and prayed for a smooth ride. She should have been more specific in her conversations with the Lord. Doris's stomach roiled. "The glare is too strong, Sheryl. I can't identify the planes. Should we take cover?"

Medic Sheryl King accompanied her to care for the injured men during the return trip. Face ashen, she stared at the sky for a long moment. "Months have passed since the Jerries did any serious bombing. Do you think they're back at it?"

"I hope not. The incident when Dr. McCann and I saw the lone bomber was frightening enough." She shuddered and tightened her grip on the steering wheel. Visions of Ron's muscular form shielding her in the culvert edged into her consciousness. Her throat thickened, and her heart beat faster. "I can't imagine experiencing a full raid." She pushed the memories to the back of her mind and craned her neck to examine the planes through the windshield.

"No sirens have activated, so we must be in the clear."

The aircraft banked, and the red-white-and-blue rondel of the RAF appeared on the bottom of the wings. Tears sprang to Doris's eyes, and she blinked them away. *Thank you, Father God.*

Sheryl rubbed her arms and flopped back against the seat. "Truth be told, I will never get used to the sound of airplane engines. When I get home, I'm going to take the train when I travel."

Doris let out a shaky laugh and pressed on the accelerator. "We're all nervous Nellies. I don't know how the British people have remained so stalwart through all of this. I've only been here a few weeks, and I'm a mess."

"Maybe they've gotten used to it."

"How could anyone do that? Wondering if your next moment will be your last or whether you'll see your family again at the end of the day."

"Don't be so macabre. So what if you don't know how long you've got to live? If I'm going to die young, I may as well have a good time before I go. You know? Eat, drink, and be merry…and all that jazz."

"I don't think condoning carousing is the idea behind the saying."

"Don't be such a wet blanket, Doris." Sheryl's face darkened. "You're such a do-gooder, but that doesn't give you the right to judge others."

"I'm—"

"You may not think so, but disdain is written all over your face."

Doris gaped at Sheryl. How had the conversation degenerated so quickly? Did she criticize people and push her beliefs? She slumped behind the wheel. "Gee, Sheryl. I'm sorry to make you feel bad. I'm the last person who has a right to condemn others. I make mistakes all the time—our discussion a case in point. Will you forgive me?"

Sheryl's glare faltered, and she shrugged. "Sure. I shouldn't have gotten so hot under the collar. Maybe that near miss stirred me up more than I thought." Shifting in her seat, she pointed at a stone Elizabethan manor perched on a rise in the distance. "Is that our destination?"

"Yes. These British country homes are something to behold, aren't they?"

"A house big enough to see from miles away. Two or three of these would hold the entire town I'm from."

"Estates are kind of like a village unto themselves. I wonder how the gentry feel about having to give up their places."

"If they're rich enough, these mansions are second homes." Sheryl giggled. "Maybe I'll find me a wealthy baron or lord and stay in England. I could get used to living in a castle with lots of staff."

"You'd have your work cut out for you with repairs. Think about what we've done at Heritage Hall converting it to useable space for a hospital. Have you heard the rumors about the damage that troops are doing to some of the homes that serve as barracks?" She grinned. "Be sure to select a guy whose place is move-in ready."

"Good advice." Sheryl snorted a laugh then cocked her head. "What do barons do for a living? Do they have an actual job like a teacher or a lawyer?"

"How much coffee did you have this morning?" Doris gave her a sidelong glance. "I've lost count of the number of topics we've covered, and we've only been on the road for thirty minutes."

"Sorry. I'm always like this. My brain hops around like a snowshoe hare. The first-aid training through the Red Cross is the first program I've succeeded in finishing."

"Congratulations. And now you're in England. I didn't know what I'd end up doing after school, but the idea of working on trucks overseas didn't enter my mind."

"Before joining the Red Cross, I'd never been out of the town where I grew up. As terrible as the war is, it has given me opportunities I might not have had."

"You mean like finding a well-to-do English earl?"

"Or an intelligent dreamboat of a doctor."

"Make up your mind."

Sheryl poked her. "I meant for you. I see the way you act around each other, studiously pretending to be casual acquaintances."

"There's nothing to fake about being acquaintances. We attended the same high school. He was a senior when I was a freshman."

"And now you're all grown up."

"That's what he said…well, after he finally recognized me."

"So, he's noticed you. That's a good sign, but you've got to reel him in, sister. You can't leave the relationship to chance."

"What relationship? There isn't one. He made that clear the last time we drove back from London. "

"Uh-huh. You keep telling yourself that fib."

Doris's heart constricted. "Besides, even if I wanted to be his gal, I can't. He could get reassigned. Then what?"

"You'd write letters like every other couple across the globe. Or you could put in for a transfer."

"I'm not going to follow him around like a love-lost puppy. Face it, a serious relationship during war is a bad idea. Even if he doesn't move. What if he gets killed?" Her voice cracked. "I couldn't handle it if something happened to him." She straightened her spine. "No, it's better not to get involved."

"Good luck with that, sister. Your words say no, but your expression definitely says yes."

Chapter Fifteen

Raucous laughter filtered across the grassy expanse between the garage and the hospital. Doris ducked out from under the hood of the ambulance and stared at the crowd of people on the lawn. She'd taken advantage of the warm, sunny day and moved the vehicle from the building to work on it. The nurses must have felt the same way about the weather and brought the many patients outside. Their joy was palpable.

Several men in wheelchairs clustered together watching two orderlies play catch. A pair of men on crutches sauntered along the lane that led to the vegetable garden. A group of patients whose arms were casted kicked a soccer ball among themselves while nurses waved their arms and reprimanded them. Each time a man successfully kept one of the women from grabbing the ball, the others cheered.

Doris shook her head. If the men felt good enough to roughhouse, why spoil the fun with a lecture? With minor injuries like broken arms or wrists, the soldiers would surely be called back to combat. They deserved some lighthearted fun before their reentry into a world of killing.

She sighed and returned her attention to the engine compartment. Gawking at the men and women in the yard wouldn't get her work finished, but the sight had brought back memories of the picnics and church fellowships she'd frequented at home. With a large percentage of boys in the armed forces and gals in the auxiliary ranks, the events were no doubt sparsely attended. Who remained? The last community newsletter issued by Mrs. Warne indicated the town was primarily women and the elderly.

Another peek at the merriment, and she froze, her gaze riveted to the tall, broad-shouldered figure. Sunshine lightened his sandy-brown hair to blonde, but the white-coated form belonged to Ron. Of that she was sure. Her heart bumped, and she chided herself for her schoolgirl reaction.

He moved among the men, bending to speak to those who couldn't stand. His face shone as he smiled and responded to his patients. He wagged his finger at the soccer players then said something to the nurses that caused them to leave the men to their game. Sure-footed, he intercepted the ball then kicked it to one of the other participants. Jeering from one side brought more amusement, then he waved and trotted toward the men on crutches who seemed delighted to have his company.

Doris blew out a shaky breath. His care, concern, and kind treatment of the men showed his compassionate side, an aspect of his personality that rarely emerged in her presence. No. That was wrong. He'd been gentle and considerate with her on occasion. Only when he was under pressure did he get testy, and who could blame him for that?

Good thing Sheryl wasn't here. That girl would know immediately that Doris was more than a little attracted to the good doctor and would never let her hear the end of it. She yanked her handkerchief from her pocket and wiped the perspiration that had formed along her hairline. Perhaps she should work inside where she wouldn't be distracted. Right. As if not seeing him would prevent her from thinking about him.

Ron raised his hand in greeting and started toward her.

Great. She'd been caught staring like a toddler in a candy store. She swallowed, her throat suddenly dry. Had he received word of his transfer? Should she ask or pretend their conversation in the truck never occurred?

Aware of her disheveled appearance, she forced a smile and tucked away the hanky. Hopefully, she didn't look too awful and sweat stained, or with any luck, didn't smell like a men's locker room.

"Nice to see the guys enjoying the lovely weather." She gestured toward the patients.

"Yes, Sister Greene was concerned they'd overexert themselves, but sunshine and clean air rarely cause a problem. Wouldn't you agree?" His deep voice rumbled.

"Uh...sure, but that's an uneducated opinion. You're the professional."

He ran his fingers over his scalp, leaving his hair spiked.

She resisted the urged to smooth the tufts. "So...uh—"

"Listen—"

They laughed in unison, and he motioned for her to continue talking.

"No, you first. I didn't have anything important to say."

"All right." He shuffled his feet and cleared his throat. "I wanted to apologize for the other day when I belittled your feelings. Saying you had no right to be upset was out of line and uncalled for. I should have handled the situation differently." He reached for her hand. "I hope you'll forgive me."

Her fingers trembled in the warmth of his palm as tingles shot up her arm. Did he feel the electricity or was she imagining the sensation? "Of course I forgive you. I'm sorry for my own behavior. We're at war. Not all information is for public consumption. I promise to remember the need for privacy in the future."

His face split into a wide smile, and he squeezed her hand. "I appreciate your grace and hope you'll pray for me as I try to be a better man. More open to change, especially where you ladies are involved. Regardless of what I manage to blurt out, I am impressed with the work all the gals do around the world. I respect you and the others. Please, believe me."

Doris peered into his eyes. Clouded with doubt, they searched her face. She shrugged. "I'll try, but you must admit some of your comments make trust difficult."

"I know. I'm a stick-in-the-mud. Opinionated and bossy. High-handed and dictatorial." He broke off and grinned. "Feel free to stop me at any time."

"No need." She giggled, and some of the tension cleared. "You're doing fine on your own."

"My sister has been telling me to change since we were kids. My dad was protective in an overbearing kind of way, and I guess I learned those behaviors from him, but I need to pave my own path now. Figure out who I am...my own convictions."

"A commendable goal."

"More difficult than I imagined. I'm finding that old habits die hard." His face reddened. "As evidenced by the other day. I really am sorry for being such an oaf."

"It's okay...well, not for being an oaf, your apology...I accept, and we'll say no more about it because God is working on me, too. You've been the recipient of the sharp side of my tongue numerous times. My temper gets the best of me, and I say things I shouldn't. I also need forgiveness and will try to be less...uh..."

"Spirited?" He chuckled and stroked the back of her hand with his thumb.

She shivered, and her breath hitched. "Generous choice of words."

He drew her into a quick hug then released her. "I'm glad things are repaired between us and to celebrate...how about if we go on a picnic? I'll take care of everything. How does that sound?"

"Afraid I'll tell your sister how awful you've been?" Doris chortled. "Or worse, your mom? Did you forget your own mother is a Rosie the Riveter at the airplane plant in town? She'd be disappointed at your attitude."

"I know. I'll give you fifty bucks not to say anything." He made a pretense at pulling money from his back pocket then widened his eyes. "I guess I left my wallet elsewhere."

"Aha! Then I can't make any promises." Their banter warmed her, and she smiled. Why couldn't their friendship be like this all the time? "Or perhaps you've got a better offer?"

He rubbed his jaw. "Hmmm. I'll have to work on my proposition…uh…proposal…" His face flamed to the roots of his hair.

"Keep digging that hole, mister. I mean, Doctor." She laughed.

"Enjoying my discomfort, are you?"

"Absolutely."

He guffawed and shook his head. "You are a pistol. I hope you'll settle for the picnic at the moment, m'lady, and I'll see what I can do to make up for my past mistakes."

"Gifts would be a good place to start. Chocolate, flowers, you know, the usual items that ladies like."

His lips quirked. "I'll keep that in mind. Now, I've kept you from your duties long enough. Will six o'clock work with your schedule? I can come by the barracks to pick you up."

Her stomach buzzed as if a swarm of bees had taken flight. "Six o'clock is perfect." Hopefully, she'd have an appetite by then.

Chapter Sixteen

Light from the setting sun filtered through the trees, casting an orange-and-pink glow over the grassy knoll. Ron grabbed a chicken drumstick from the basket and nibbled on the succulent meat while Doris pushed food around on the plate. His medical instincts kicked in. Was she not feeling well but too embarrassed to admit it? Her color was good, and she hadn't seemed extra warm as if feverish when he picked her up.

His chest tightened. Maybe she regretted her decision to have dinner with him by the pond. Perhaps she'd accepted his invitation too quickly and now wondered how long she had to keep him company. Granted, he wasn't as suave as some of the other guys, but he could at least entertain her for a bit. They'd gotten along all right on the periodic trips to other hospitals. Surely, he could prove himself to be somewhat fun to be around.

He pressed his lips against a sigh. "Is the food not to your liking?"

Her head jerked up, and she met his gaze with wide eyes. "What? Oh, no…it's delicious."

"Is that why you keeping poking at it?"

She set down the plate, and pressed a hand on her stomach. Her face flamed, giving her an appearance of guilt. "Can I be honest?"

Brace yourself, boy. Here it comes. Ron forced a smile. "Of course. I'd expect nothing less."

She patted her hair then tightened her pony tail, and his eyes were drawn to her silky tresses. What he wouldn't give to pull out the band that held her dark locks in place. To watch it swish onto her shoulders. To run his hands through its glossy smoothness.

"...so that's all. I hope you understand." She rubbed her hands on her skirt.

Uh oh. He'd been so caught up in her beauty, he missed what she'd said. What an idiot. Now, he'd have to fake his response. "Absolutely." He nibbled the inside of his cheek. What had he agreed to?

Relief coursed over Doris's face, and she blew out a deep breath. "Thanks. I'm being silly, I know, but I haven't been on many dates...uh...not that this is a date, but I usually pal around with the girls, and that's different. You know what I mean?"

It sounded like she was nervous about being on the picnic. With him. Alone. She wasn't the only one who was skittish. "Yeah, but we've got shared history, which is more than most folks who wind up over here. We can talk about the good old days."

A giggle like tinkling wind chimes escaped her lips, and she cocked her head, eyebrows arched high on her forehead. "The good old days when a lofty senior boy had little time for a gawky, freshman girl."

He chuckled. "Okay, so maybe the only thing shared in our past was location, but we can talk about that. Will it make you too homesick? We're here to have fun not depress each other."

"I don't think talking about home will bother me, or maybe, in a bittersweet way. I mean, even though we're here because of a war, I'm getting to do work that is challenging and exciting in a field I couldn't break into at home. I miss some things, but in a weird way, I'm not anxious to go back, well, except when we get bombed." She shuddered. "I could do without Hitler's flying henchmen, but we've been blessed thus far, not getting injured."

"Your optimism is one of the things I lo—appreciate about you."

She ducked her head. "My sisters say I'm an idealist as if it's a bad trait."

"I disagree." He picked up another chicken leg. "You first. What do you miss about home?"

"Well…" She looked into the distance and tapped her index finger on her chin. A grin lit up her face. "Roller skating at Gadaway Park, speeding around the bandstand as if I were flying or riding a horse. The wind in my hair. I felt free…unencumbered, as if I were actually graceful, not gangly and clumsy."

"You? Clumsy? I can't see it."

"Again, you weren't looking. Too busy doing your own thing."

He swallowed against the lump that formed in his throat. "High school is awful for most of us, isn't it? Trying to figure out who we are while attempting to fit in with a bunch of kids who have no idea who they are, many of whom lash out in meanness as a way to feel better about themselves. Ugh."

"To be honest, it wasn't much better in college, part of the reason I dropped out." She waved her hand. "Your turn. What do you miss?"

"Promise you won't laugh?"

"Never."

"Okay…feeding the fish with my dad off the dam."

"Really?"

He shrugged. "Sounds stupid saying it out loud."

"No. Time with family is never dumb. I saw you a couple of times."

Tears pricked the backs of his eyes. "Good memories. He was so busy, but for some reason he would make time about once a month to head over to the dam, and he always asked me to accompany him. Precious times. Just the two of us." He cleared his throat. "He died of a heart attack two weeks before I graduated from med school."

She squeezed his hand then left her fingers nestled in his palm. "He was proud of your accomplishments. I'd run into him in town sometimes, and he'd regale me with your grades and tell me what you were doing." A single tear trickled down her cheek, and she swiped it away. "Maybe we can find a school of fish who need feeding."

"I'd like that." He wiped his hands on a napkin then pointed to her empty plate. "Your appetite returned. That's good. One shouldn't leave a picnic hungry."

"Yes, talking about home made me forget my nervousness. The food was delicious. How did you manage to get your hands on fried chicken and coleslaw?"

Ron chuckled. "One of the cooks owed me a favor. They're serving it for dinner tonight, and he said there was more than enough to go around."

"I hate to ask what kind of favor."

"It's best left unsaid." He dug into his breast coat pocket and pulled out a paperback. "Have you seen these? The military is calling them armed services editions. They plan to publish hundreds so the boys will have something to read during their downtime. The Victory Book Campaign worked out okay, but the cost of shipping all those hardbacks was exorbitant. And a lot of the books were unsuitable—stuff no one wanted to read."

Doris reached for the book. "*Oliver Twist*. I love Dickens. What a wonderful idea. The logistics of taking care of our troops must be overwhelming. I hadn't thought about keeping them entertained."

"Can you imagine going on a ten-mile march carrying a hardback copy of *Great Expectations*?"

"I expect I'd toss it by the roadside. How did you get your hands on the book? Another favor?"

He shook his head. "Nope, swapped it for a Louis L'Amour from my own library."

"I didn't figure you for a reader of western stories." Doris cocked her head. "I wonder what else I don't know about you." She flipped to the first page, and he leaned forward to read over her shoulder. A stray lock of her hair brushed his cheek, and he sucked in a breath. With effort, he read aloud, "Among other public buildings in a certain town, which for many reasons it will be prudent to refrain from mentioning, and to which I will assign no fictitious name, there is one anciently common to most towns, great or small: to wit, a workhouse; and in this workhouse was born; on a day and date which I need not trouble myself to repeat, inasmuch as it can be of no possible consequence to the reader, in this stage of the business at all events; the item of mortality whose name is prefixed to the head of this chapter."

She closed the book. "That's got to be the world's longest first sentence, don't you think? I do love it, though…sets the stage for the entire book."

He drew back. "He was a great writer, whereas I can barely string together two words."

"Doesn't matter. Patching up our guys good as new is more important."

"Not really, just a different set of skills." He glanced at his watch. Drat. Time to return for his shift. Where had the evening gone? "Unfortunately, I've got to get back."

"Me, too. When you're done I'd like to borrow the book."

"Or we could read it together." He searched her face. Would she be amenable to the idea?

Her eyes sparkled, and she nodded. "I'd like that."

His chest swelled, and he rose and helped her to her feet. "Wonderful. Is tomorrow too soon?"

"I'll have to check my schedule."

His heart fell. "You may be booked already?"

"Yeah, I may have to perform surgery on some poor ambulance." She laughed and began to collect their soiled dishes and put them into the basket. "The mileage on the vehicles adds up quickly, and the wear and tear occurs sooner than normal."

"Ah, of course." His chest lightened. The breeze picked up and lifted one of the cloth napkins like a kite, sending it skittering across the meadow. He gave chase and snatched it from the air.

She applauded. "I've not seen you run that fast before. Didn't know you had it in you."

He executed a deep bow then trotted toward her. "Very funny. Guess I'm full of surprises today. Like this one." He rolled the napkin and snapped it at her, not quite hitting her arm.

Her mouth formed a perfect O, then a wicked grin curved her lips. She reached into the basket for the other napkin. In a flash, she thwacked his arm with the cloth, then danced away, her laughter triumphant.

"Hey!" He raced toward her, and she shrieked as her legs pounded to keep away from his reach. Breathless, he caught up with her and grabbed her arm. He swung her around, and she pressed against him, heart bumping in rhythm with his. Her pupils dilated, and she pinked. His gaze went to her lips, so close. So kissable.

With a loud squawk, a large raven swooped onto the blanket.

Doris sprang out of his arms then waved her hands at the bird. "Hey, get away from that." The winged creature protested the interruption with another raucous call then raised its wings and took flight.

Ron shook his head. So much for their special moment.

Chapter Seventeen

Doris's cheeks burned as if she'd spent a day at the beach. Why did she have to blush at the smallest provocation? The crow was a welcome disturbance. If Ron's expression were any indication, he intended to kiss her. She touched her lips. Gaze fixed on her mouth, his eyes had darkened to a glittering cobalt.

Mouth dry and heart throbbing, she blinked. Get hold of yourself, Doris. He's a cliché. Tall, dark, and handsome. Granted, he's no Cary Grant, but he gives the actor a run for his money with his dimpled chin, broad shoulders, and rugged appearance. Sharp wit and intelligence sweetened the package.

How many girls had he taken out or kissed in the months since arriving in England? The British girls were starved for affection, weren't they? Their men were off at war. The Americans were plentiful and well paid. Ron was a long way from home and lonely. Or maybe she was jumping to conclusions, and he was just trying to make up for being a boor, like he said. To ensure she didn't send any scathing reports to her folks. Or his.

Basket in hand, she marched to the jeep while he folded the blanket. He claimed to have dated few women during college, but perhaps that was merely a story, one to set her at ease and try to lull her into a false sense of security. Yes, he was arrogant, but he didn't prey on women. He'd been taught better than that.

She stumbled over a divot in the ground, her ankle twisting. Righting herself, Doris continued to the vehicle. Had Ron seen her clumsiness? Seen that she was the same lanky, awkward girl she'd been in high school?

Footsteps pounded the ground behind her as Ron trotted to catch up. "Hey, I would have carried that. You left me with the lightweight work."

Lifting the basket into the back of the jeep, she forced a smile. "There's little remaining inside. We ate everything."

He nudged her shoulder. "You mean *I* ate everything."

A chuckle escaped, and she smoothed her slacks. She needed time to recover from his nearness. *Lord, I don't know what to do. My emotions are all jumbled. One minute I'm sure he cares about me more than as a friend, and the next I've contrived myriad ulterior motives for him. What do I do?* She cleared her throat. "I didn't want to hurt your feelings."

"Since when?" He stuffed the blanket into the back of the jeep then brushed off his hands and crooked his elbow. "M'lady, may I escort you to your seat?"

So, he had seen her ungainliness. She sighed and slid her hand into his arm. She would play along. "Thank you, fair knight."

His face split into a wide grin, and he patted her hand, sending tingles through her fingers that zinged up her arm. He led her to the passenger side of the jeep, and she climbed into the vehicle. "Are you comfortable, m'lady?"

"Yes, thank you." How long was he going to keep up the role? A stiff breeze swept past, and a stray lock of hair tumbled over her face. Before she could tuck the errant strand behind her ear, he reached forward capturing the tresses between his fingers. "You have the most beautiful hair I've ever seen. Gold and red highlights cause it to shimmer in the light." He took a deep breath. "And your hair always smells so fresh. Floral, but not quite."

Her toes curled, and she gaped at him, eyes wide. He was no longer playing. "Uh…thank you."

He draped the tendril over her ear then ran his finger along her jawline.

She shivered at his touch.

Face angled toward her, he leaned into the jeep and lowered his mouth to hers, his lips warm on hers. He deepened the kiss, and unbidden, her arms snaked around his neck drawing him closer. His musky scent filled her nose. Too soon, he pulled away then pressed a kiss on her forehead and each cheek. "As much as I hate to, we need to return to the hospital. Being late wouldn't be fair to Dr. Frankel. He works too many hours as it is."

"Yes, I understand." Heart banging against her ribs, she crossed her arms to prevent the offending organ from jumping out of her chest. "I should get back as well." Her words sounded terse in her ears, and she cringed. Would she have enough time to regain her composure? Or would Sheryl take one look at her and know she'd been kissed?

His smile sagged, and he tapped the tip of her nose. "Right, let's get to it, then." He walked around the jeep and slid behind the wheel. Turning the key, he brought the engine to life.

They bumped along the broken macadam, and Doris gripped the dashboard to keep from being pitched out of her seat. She peeked at him through her peripheral vision and hunched into herself. Was his wooden expression instigated by her words or her inexperienced kiss?

**

Ron's grip tightened on the steering wheel as he fought for composure. He was perspiring as if he'd run a marathon, and his pulse was at tachycardia rates. Would his foolishness bring on a heart attack? He rubbed his chest and forced himself to take a deep breath.

What had he been thinking when he kissed Doris? He rolled his eyes. He hadn't been thinking. At all. He let his emotions get the better of him, and before he knew what was good for him, he'd kissed her. Kissed her for all he was worth.

Perfect. Now she'd really think he was a jerk. That he'd taken advantage of her. The miracle was that she hadn't slapped him. Instead, multiple emotions—surprise, embarrassment, regret, and possibly revulsion—washed over her face. Her porcelain face with its smattering of tiny freckles that danced across her nose.

She cleared her throat, and his gaze shot toward her. She opened her mouth as if to say something but then pressed her lips together. Was she trying to choose the exact words to berate him for his behavior? Maybe he should help her out.

"Listen—"

"Ron—"

"You first." He patted her shoulder, and she flinched. His heart dropped. Did she fear him?

"Okay…uh…Why did you kiss me?"

"What?"

"I need to know why you kissed me. We're not dating. In fact, we're barely friends, bickering more than getting along."

"I'm sorry. I shouldn't have. You're angry. It won't happen again."

"No, not angry, mostly confused." She turned so she faced him. "You didn't answer my question."

"Okay. Can I be honest with you?"

She pierced him with a steely gaze. "I'd expect nothing less, but does that mean you haven't been?"

His face heated. "No, of course not. I may be an excellent surgeon, but I'm completely out of my element with women. With you. You're beautiful, smart, funny…I get all tied up in knots and nerves when we're together. I want to make a good impression, but instead I usually put my foot in my mouth." He cocked his head. "I'm attracted to you. Don't you feel the electricity between us? You seemed to respond, at least for a moment."

"Look, Ron, you're a nice guy—"

"Oh, no. Not the 'nice guy' speech." He braked the jeep and turned off the engine. "Really, you don't feel something…anything?"

"Whether I do or not isn't the point." She studied her hands as if they were the most interesting things she'd ever seen. "Others might be willing to pursue a relationship during the war, but I'm not. Besides, we can't even call whatever we're doing a relationship."

He grabbed her hands, and they froze under his palm. "Now, who's avoiding the question? I deserve to know whether or not you have feelings for me…and not those as a friend or brother. Please. I was honest with you. Can you at least do the same for me?"

Doris blew out a loud breath and met his eyes. "Fine. Honestly, my emotions for you run the gamut. On our good days, you treat me with respect and make me laugh. You challenge me to think smarter and harder. Then there are the times you belittle my ideas or act like you're the only one of us who has any brains. I wake up in the morning wanting to see you and talk to you, at the same time dreading which of your personalities has clocked in at work."

She shrugged. "There are too many unknowns in my life, the biggest one being whether you or I will live to see another day. Hitler will continue to bomb England until she rolls over or gets the best of him.

You're considering a transfer. If I open my heart, it could get broken, with or without your intending to. I'm not willing to risk that." She rubbed her forehead. "Can we please just go back to the hospital?"

"Sure." His voice was barely above a whisper. Gray clouds rolled across the sky as if God were mourning with him. As soon as he got to the office, he'd call the director and accept the transfer. Doris obviously didn't want him around, so he'd grant her wish even though his heart shattered at the thought.

Chapter Eighteen

Doris guided the ambulance through the debris-filled town of Watford outside London. Young and old, uniformed and civilian worked together clearing rubble off sidewalks and streets. Fortunately, the air raid had been somewhat unsuccessful with most of the bombs falling in the forest and meadows, but an entire block had been decimated, and the small, local hospital was overflowing with injured. Ron agreed to house some of the patients until another solution could be found.

Ron. His face sprang to mind, and she pushed the image away. She had work to do, and his presence would distract her. If only she could get her heart to cooperate with her mind.

Dust clung to the air and coated the windshield. If bombs didn't kill the population, lung ailments from breathing in the particles might do Hitler's dirty work.

Sheryl pointed to the detour indicated by hand-painted signs, and Doris nodded. She squeezed the vehicle through the tight lane surrounded by piles of bricks, broken plaster, and shattered wood. Resolute expressions painted every face. The acrid smell of coal filtered through the cracks in the ambulance.

At the end of the street, an Air Raid Precaution worker motioned for her to turn right. A glance to the left showed a house half-blown away, the other half leaning like a macabre version of the Tower of Pisa. Doris shuddered.

Ten minutes later, she spotted their destination and pulled into the parking lot, eerily vacant of all but ambulances or military vehicles, a reminder that very few citizens had cars or fuel to fill them. She lined up behind a queue of other ambulances and surveyed the area.

Despite the annihilation around it, the hospital stood undamaged, no bricks out of place, an oasis in the midst of destruction. A pair of white-coated orderlies carried a stretcher to the back of the lead vehicle. A nurse bent over the patient. She patted the wounded man's shoulder then stepped away so the workers could climb in and settle the injured man. The driver slammed the hatch, slid behind the wheel, and drove off, leaving space for the line to inch forward.

Like precision clockwork, eight more orderlies with patients swarmed the next ambulance and fastened the four stretchers in place before rushing into the building for more. A tall, sandy-haired man, with a stethoscope draped around his neck, jogged down the stairs. He carried a sheaf of papers and made his way to the nurse at the curb. Doris's heart tripped. The doctor was a dead ringer for Ron. Or was it Ron?

She squinted through the windshield and sighed. Her mother would say she was jumping at shadows.

"Hey, that guy could be your Dr. Dreamy. Don't you think?" Sheryl waved toward the man Doris had been studying.

"He's not mine, and you've got to stop calling him Dr. Dreamy. One of these days, you're going to address him like that to his face, and then where will you be?"

Sheryl giggled. "What's the harm in letting him know I think he's a looker? Although, with that ego of his, he doesn't need any encouragement."

"Just change the subject, okay?" Doris accelerated, and the ambulance rolled forward. She braked a short distance from the vehicle in front of her. If she didn't get Sheryl focused on another topic, they'd spend the entire return trip with her speculating about Ron, and there'd be no way for Doris to get him out of her head.

"Whatever you say." Sheryl executed a mock salute then gestured toward a pair of orderlies waiting to load their patient. "What about that guy? He's cute. With any luck, he'll be one of ours."

"What is with you and ogling at all the men? We're here to do a job."

"Except right now all we're doing is sitting in a queue waiting, so there's nothing wrong with me admiring the scenery." She stroked her jaw. "What about that one? Maybe I should put in a transfer to work here."

Doris rolled her eyes. "You're incorrigible. Will you put in for a transfer each time you get bored with the…uh…scenery?"

"Nah. I talk a good game, but I like working at Heritage Hall with you and the other gals." She crossed her arms and slumped against the seat. "I moved a lot when I was growing up. It was hard being new girl on the block every couple of years. Kids are tough on each other, and I got picked on."

"Why did you pick the Medical Corps? They can keep moving you around."

"Yeah, but they move all of us, and we end up stationed together at some point. Granted, I didn't think about the transfers when I joined up, but so far, it has worked out. What about you? Why the Red Cross? You're an ace mechanic. Don't you have your pick of jobs?"

"Not at home. Nobody seems to want a female grease monkey. In a weird way, the war has been one of the best things to happen to me. I've had opportunities I never would have back in New Hampshire. The job hasn't been all roses, but I'm doing what I love with people I enjoy." Doris winked. "Even you."

"Hey—"

"Now's your chance." Doris rolled the ambulance forward, now first in line. "Go get 'em, girl." She spied Ron's doppelganger still on the sidewalk. "I'll wait here. You don't need my assistance."

"Thanks." Sheryl gave her a thumbs-up and jumped out of the vehicle, slamming the door behind her.

Doris chuckled. The medic was a character and acted like a cat on the prowl, but Doris knew she was all talk. The eight-by-ten glossy of her boyfriend on the wall above her bunk, and the wallet-sized duplicate she carried told a different story. She was crazy in love with her young man. Pretending to be on the lookout for a new guy probably chased away some of her blues and loneliness.

At least she had someone special. Doris touched her lips. With a bit of encouragement, it seemed she could, too. But she'd blown it when she told Ron she had no feelings. Ron's downcast eyes and hurt expression were evidence they'd passed the point of no return.

She studied the doctor who resembled Ron. A good-looking man, to be sure, but his jaw wasn't as square nor his shoulders as broad. And his hair receded on either side of his forehead. He gestured to something as he spoke to the nurse, and a wedding band glinted in the sun. Doris's face heated. The man was married. Shame on her for examining him like a choice cut of meat. *Forgive me, God.*

The back hatch slammed, rocking the ambulance. Sheryl appeared at the window then opened the door and climbed inside.

"Don't you have to stay with the patients?"

"Nope, one of the nurses here got a forty-eight-hour pass, and we're giving her a lift. Apparently, her sister lives near our hospital. As a way to return the favor, she offered to ride with the boys."

"Excellent." Doris put the ambulance in gear and drove toward the exit. "It will be nice to have the company on the drive."

"Even if I want to talk about Dr. Dreamy." Sheryl guffawed. "As if you could stop me. Did you get an eyeful of that guy who looks like him? Handsome but not nearly as attractive. Don't you think?"

"He's married."

"What?" She whipped her head toward the man who was disappearing into the building then turned to stare at Doris. "How did you…wait…you totally checked him out, didn't you? You act all high and mighty, but you're as bad as the rest of us." She slapped her knee. "Don't try to deny it. There's no other way you'd know about his marital status."

"Okay, I admit it." She shrugged. "I couldn't help it. He was standing right in front of the vehicle."

"Yeah, that's the reason. Good for you. But what I really need the skinny on is you and Dr.—"

"Don't say it."

"McCann." Eyes wide in mock confusion, Sheryl grinned. "I was going to say McCann."

"Right. And I'm Mrs. Roosevelt." She nudged her friend's shoulder. "Get serious. I do want to talk to you about him."

Sheryl bolted upright. "Something happened. What happened? I know you went on a picnic. Did he kiss you? He kissed you, didn't he?"

"Yes."

"I knew it." Squealing, Sheryl waved her hands in the air. "You've been skittish about him for a couple of days. Tell me everything."

Doris filled her in about the last two days, talking faster and faster as she recounted the events. It was as if now she had someone to share with, the geyser had let loose. "You see, I ruined it by what I said, so it doesn't matter how cute or nice he is. I've hurt his feelings. There's no reason for him to pursue a relationship even if we could."

"Silly, just apologize. He'll take you back. He's got to."

"Why?"

"Well…I don't know…the two of you would be swell together. That's why." She flounced against the seat.

"I'm not sure I want him to. There's a war on. What if one of us gets transferred or wounded or killed. I don't want to start something I can't finish. Yes, he's wonderful, and it's breaking my heart to choose not to see him, but we should be friends, only friends. I've got a job to do. He's got a job to do."

"Honey, you can't wall off yourself from love because it might not work out. What if you turn your back on this, and it could have been the best thing to ever happen to you? You know, except for the fact that you get to work on cars and trucks. That's cool."

"Funny."

"I'm a regular riot, aren't I?" Sheryl batted her eyelashes. "Look, I don't think there's much more I can say about this. You know your choices. Personally, I think it would be a shame if you didn't try to work out things with Dr. Dre—McCann, but it's not my decision." She glanced at her watch. "Now, I'm going out with some of the gals tonight, and I want to be at my best, so I'm going to catch some shut-eye. Wake me when we get there."

"You're not going to listen to my side?"

"Nope."

"You really think I'm making a bad choice."

"Yep." She pulled the bill of her cap over her face then crossed her arms and stretched her legs.

Doris sighed and gripped the wheel as the vehicle bounced over the washboard road. The rhythm mesmerized her. I love him. I love him not. I love him. I love him not.

Miles passed, and they entered the wrought-iron gate that had somehow been missed during the regular scrap drives. She poked Sheryl then followed the lane to the hospital.

Sheryl sat up and yawned then wiggled her eyebrows and gave her a sly grin.

Ron stood on the gravel talking to Sister Greene. He looked up and waved, a crooked smile lighting up his face.

Doris's heart melted. So much for her resolve to stay unencumbered.

Chapter Nineteen

Doris tossed the wrench into the metal toolbox with a clank then pulled a rag from her pocket and wiped her hands. It felt good to be back at Heritage Hall after a week away. When she returned from transporting patients from Hatfield House, she found orders assigning her to another hospital for a week. One of their mechanics had fallen ill with appendicitis and a second had been killed in a bombing raid. Some days the war was too close for comfort.

She rotated her neck to ease the stiffness from being bent over the engine compartment of the ambulance. Nice to get the tune-up finished before the end of her shift which meant no one would have to take over. The other girls had done a great job of covering for her while she was gone, and they hadn't complained about the longer hours, but she wanted to pull her weight.

With a nod of satisfaction, she slammed the hood, and the bang reverberated in the cavernous garage. The process of taking out each part, cleaning it or replacing it…some people might find the tasks tedious, but not her. She hummed Tommy Dorsey's latest song while she put away the rest of her tools and straightened up the workbench. A final swipe at the surface with her rag, and she was done. Brushing the dust off her coveralls, she turned to leave and froze.

Ron stood about ten feet away, hat in hand.

Her heart plummeted, and she pressed a hand on her chest. "You startled me. How did I not hear you arrive?"

He chuckled. "Don't you know by now that you get lost in your work. You tend to block out the rest of the world when you're performing surgery on a vehicle. A bit like myself. I appreciate that kind of passion." He fiddled with the brim of his hat. "May I walk you home…er…back to your barracks? We left things awkwardly, and I don't want it to be like that with us."

Maybe she hadn't hurt him as badly as she thought. Or maybe he was a great actor. Or maybe he was a kind and gracious man willing to give her a second chance. No matter what the reason, she was glad he'd come around to see her.

Hard to admit, but she'd missed him. Badly. The week at the other location had been exciting. Different vehicles to work on, some of which she'd never seen, meaning she'd had the challenge of learning about new parts, layout, and engineering. But at the end of each shift she went to the dining hall alone, bolted down her meal, and tried not to look for a certain handsome doctor who wasn't there. She may as well face it: she enjoyed time with him, no matter how often her head cautioned her heart to back away.

Aware of her appearance and pungent odor, she cringed. Would she be able to stay downwind of Ron? If he thought their last conversation was awkward, wait until he got a whiff of her on the way to the barracks. Should she turn him down to prevent embarrassment for them both or just give him fair warning?

His smile wavered, and he ran his fingers through his hair. "I'm sorry. Did you have plans? I shouldn't have assumed you were free."

"No." She held up her hand. "That's not it. I've...uh...been working, and I'm not exactly fresh as a daisy. Are you sure you want to be close to me?" Her face warmed. Great. Now she'd drawn attention to how dirty and unfeminine she was. She wouldn't have to worry about him wanting to pursue a relationship after all. If she was lucky, he'd still want to be friends at a minimum, but perhaps after she'd showered.

"As a physician, I'm not put off by a little bit of perspiration."

"How about a lot?"

He threw back his head and laughed. Long and hard.

Her cheeks heated even more, and she scowled. "Are you making fun of me?"

"Absolutely not." Still smiling, he crooked his elbow. "I'd be honored to walk you home if you'll allow me."

Doris shook her head. "I'll walk with you but without any contact."

"Fair enough, but there's no need to be embarrassed." He reached over and tugged on a stray lock of hair that had tumbled from under her cap. "You're more beautiful than any gal, even after a full day at work."

"Let's keep the compliments to a minimum."

He shrugged. "Okay, but at some point I will convince you of your loveliness, both on the inside and the outside."

To avoid responding, she picked up the toolbox and set it on the bench, so it would be ready for the next shift. A quick glance around the garage told her everything else was stowed away. She'd stalled long enough. "I'm ready." She stuffed her hands into her pockets and sauntered out of the building by his side.

Ron rubbed his jaw. "Look, before we talk about anything else, I wanted you to know I've given our conversation a lot of thought, and I want to apologize for my behavior."

She opened her mouth to reply, but he held up his hand.

"You are right when you say my behavior is erratic. I don't want to be overbearing and obnoxious, but those traits keep winning out over the man I'm trying to become. Please forgive me. I'd like to be your friend, if you'll let me."

"Friends?"

"Yes. I'd like more, but you don't, so I need to respect your decision."

She tugged at the collar of her shirt that suddenly felt too tight. "I like this man better than the obnoxious one." She liked him a lot.

"Me, too."

The sun hadn't quite dropped behind the trees, and the fiery ball cast shards of orange, pink, and red across the meadows that flanked the path leading to the stone cottage that had been converted to lodging for the medics and Red Cross girls. The so-called cottage was larger than any of the mansions on the rich side of town at home. The nurses stayed in another building farther down the lane.

"This property is something else, isn't it?" Doris gestured toward the vacant stables that could easily house two dozen horses. Maybe more. "The garage is nicer than my parents' place. Do the owners use all this space?"

He nodded. "A tremendous number of staff are required for the upkeep of an estate like this. Even more were necessary in decades and centuries past when the tasks were all done by hand, without benefit of machinery."

"I didn't think about the lack of modern conveniences causing so much work. Life is easier for us, isn't it?"

"I take it your quarters are acceptable?"

"They're gorgeous. Gleaming wood floors, lovely wainscoting, and lots of windows. Spacious, too."

"Excellent. How many gals share your room?"

"Two, but one of the gals works nights, so we rarely see each other. Apparently, she's always worked the eleven-to-seven and volunteered for it as soon as she arrived."

"I don't mind nights once in a while, but I wouldn't want to make a career of it."

"Me, neither."

"If we're going to be friends, I want to tell you a bit about my history, so you're not blindsided later."

Her mouth went dry. "Should I be worried?"

"I'll let you decide." Ron nudged her shoulder. "Kidding. I'm kidding." He cleared his throat. "I was engaged once."

Doris gasped then clapped her hand over her mouth.

"You're shocked anyone would want to marry me, aren't you?" His smile took the sting from his words.

"No."

"It's okay. I'm as astounded as you, but she came to her senses before the process went too far. She's a lovely girl, and she'll make some lucky guy a wonderful wife. A man better than me. Someone who will cherish her as I should have before I let my schooling and my profession take the front seat in our relationship." He pulled at his ear. "Residency is brutal on both the doctor and his family. We work horrendous hours, often sleeping at the hospital. When we do go home, we're groggy and irascible. Phoebe grew tired of excuses as to why I was too busy to see her or help plan our wedding."

"You didn't have a choice about the hours you were putting in."

"I should have made her a priority in my life, or I shouldn't have asked her to marry me until after I'd completed the residency, and perhaps even waiting until I'd set up my practice."

"Well, it's her loss."

Ron turned toward her, his eyebrow raised. "You think I'm a catch?"

"With a little bit of work, yes."

He snorted a laugh. "Touché."

She giggled, and her palms slicked with moisture. It felt good to laugh and shed the day's stresses.

"What about you? Any boyfriends or fiancés in your past?"

"I dated occasionally but nothing serious. To be honest, most guys can't seem to get past my height."

"The male ego is a fragile thing."

"Apparently." She shot him a wry smile. "You wouldn't know anything about that, would you?"

He grabbed his chest and feigned a heart attack. "If only you knew how sensitive a guy I really am."

"I'm beginning to realize it."

They approached the cottage, and Doris quelled her disappointment. She'd enjoyed the walk more than she wanted to acknowledge. Being hurt in the past needed to stay in the past. She shouldn't let the bruises cloud her willingness to explore another relationship, but the regret in Ron's voice was heavy when he spoke about Phoebe. Was he still in love with her?

Doris wrapped her arms around her middle. "Thanks for walking me back. I'll see you…uh…sometime."

"Your forgiveness means a lot, Doris. If I keep messing up, I'm afraid you'll give up on me. I promised you we could be friends, and only friends, but I hope you'll consider something more eventually. You're an alluring, intelligent woman who takes away my breath. And you keep me on my toes. I like that." He leaned toward her, eyes glittering with desire.

Her breath caught as he pressed his mouth on hers, warm and inviting.

In an instant, his lips were gone. He touched the brim of his hat. "Good night, Doris."

Heart hammering, she stumbled inside, then closed the door and leaned against it. Was there a future with this man who infuriated her one minute and tantalized her the next?

Chapter Twenty

Doris rolled over in bed and put the pillow over her face to block out the sunshine that streamed through the window. Suffocating, she groaned and tossed the cushion away, then sat up with a yawn. Two days had passed since Ron walked her home and made his intentions clear. Forty-eight hours of avoiding him so she could figure out what she wanted, how she could juggle her job and fears with her growing feelings for him.

He'd given her space, waving from afar in the dining hall and twice outside the hospital when she caught sight of him on her way to the garage. His smile was wide and genuine, setting off twinges of guilt about her inability to make up her mind. Her stomach quivered as if the entire cast of *Swan Lake* performed inside her belly. She'd never felt like this in the past when she was sure she was in love.

Sheryl worked the last two nights so wasn't available for Doris to consult. Instead, she'd argued with herself nearly every waking moment, which had been entirely unproductive. She practically sleepwalked through her days then tossed and turned once she'd crawled into bed.

She owed Ron an explanation and sooner rather than later. His patience had to be wearing thin. Hers certainly was, and she was the culprit.

The door to the bedroom opened and hit the wall with a bang. Doris jolted.

"Sorry, Doris."

Her roommates, who both worked nights, stumbled into the room. Sleep was definitely no longer an option even if she wanted to.

"I'm getting up anyway. Anything special I should be aware of today?"

"Yeah, ambulance number three threw a rod, and number eight got a hole in the oil pan, so it needs to be replaced."

Good. A full day of challenge to keep her mind and hands occupied. She'd volunteer to handle both of them. "Thanks." She slipped from the bed, grabbed her clothes, and headed for the bathroom to change, so the exhausted girls could hit the hay immediately.

A quick fifteen minutes later, she was ready for work. She hurried out of the cottage and headed to the hospital, where she could grab a quick bite before clocking in. She wasn't very hungry, but the work required on the two malfunctioning vehicles meant she would miss lunch.

She ascended the stairs into the building then made her way toward the cafeteria. The familiar aroma of fried potatoes melded with the scent of sausage, or bangers as the British called them, wafted through the corridor. Different from the American version, she'd grown to love the spicy meat.

Half-full, the room buzzed with conversation punctuated with laughter and the clank of cutlery on metal trays. Doctors, nurses, medics, orderlies, mechanics, and administrative staff mingled regardless of hierarchy. Doris smiled. Next to working on the vehicles, the casual familiarity among the employees was her favorite thing about being stationed here.

She queued up behind a trio of nurses in the food line. They chattered like magpies while they moved forward and selected their meals. She followed along, mouthwatering at the choices. One of the cooks had made fresh biscuits, and a bowl of oranges beckoned from the tea station. The Red Cross was well connected, but she hadn't seen citrus since her arrival. The succulent fruit would go like lemonade on a hot day in Georgia.

Her tray full, she surveyed the room for an empty spot near the window so she could soak up some sun. With both vehicles out of commission, she wouldn't be able to get them outside the garage to work in the beautiful weather. In the far corner, a group of doctors rose and vacated a perfect location. She gripped her tray tighter and threaded her way through the crowd to the table then sat with a sigh.

Bowing her head, she gave thanks for the meal. *And Lord, please help me figure out what to do with my battered heart. Ron deserves an answer.* She opened her eyes then swallowed a laugh. Apparently, God thought it was time to handle the situation. Ron stood by the table, tray in hand, and a questioning look on his face.

"Would you like to join me?"

He smiled and lowered himself into the chair across from her before setting down his food. "I was hoping you'd say that." He took a swig of tea and grimaced. "As much as the British think their tea is better than coffee, I'll never agree. That's the real reason for fighting the Japs, you know. They've taken all the islands we need for coffee, rubber, and silk, but mostly coffee."

She snickered. He had such a great sense of humor. "Not me. You can have it." She speared a potato chunk and poked it into her mouth so she wouldn't have to talk. Let him carry the conversation.

Ron spread jam on his toast then piled a bit of scrambled eggs on top of the bread before taking a bite of the concoction.

"Eww. You ruined a perfectly good piece of toast with that move." She wrinkled her nose and ate more potatoes. She'd save the orange for later.

"Your problem is being a finicky eater. All the food goes the same place. What does it matter how I eat it?"

"First of all, I don't have a problem with my eating habits." She cocked her head and grinned to show she knew he was kidding. "Second, the chef would be horrified to see what you've done with his creation."

He wiped his lips with a napkin and returned her smile.

Her gaze went to his mouth, and her face warmed when she realized he noticed her attention. She took a swig of water then coughed when it went down the wrong way. Covering her mouth with a napkin, she hacked and wheezed. If she wasn't choking to death, she'd roll her eyes at herself for yet another ungraceful moment. What did he see in her?

Ron jumped up and stroked her back.

A few more coughs, then the pain in her lungs eased, and she took a tentative breath. Her throat felt like sandpaper had scraped it, but she didn't gag. She nodded. "Thanks. I'm okay."

Concern etched lines on his face. "Are you sure? I'm a doctor, you know."

"Yeah, I got that from your lightning response. You can stop rubbing my back." She jerked her head toward the diners. "They might think you've changed disciplines to massage therapy."

He dropped his hands as if scalded then chuckled. "Got me with that one. See? Keeping me on my toes." He picked up her glass. "You should take a few sips to ease the roughness in your throat."

"You really are a physician, aren't you?" She grinned and allowed him to hold the cup up to her lips. "Your medical knowledge is astounding."

"Award winning."

She took the glass from him, and their fingers brushed, sending tingles up her arm. Yeah, she had it bad, and there was no time like the present to tell him. How would her revelation change things?

Ron bent over Doris and evaluated her condition. She seemed recovered, but something was amiss. Myriad emotions flitted across her flushed face. Pink from exertion, the color was also a result of embarrassment as chagrin settled into place in her expression. His heart rate returned to normal.

She waved him back into his seat, and he acquiesced.

"Thanks. If I can't handle my drink, how am I going to manage with dangerous tools today? Could get dicey in the garage."

He loved how she tried to laugh off her discomfort, and he would play along so she could regain her composure. "Perhaps cutting gloves from the kitchen are in order. Should you call out sick...or incapacitated? I could give you a doctor's note." He pretended to pull a pen from his jacket pocket.

"Would you? That'd be great." She snickered, a musical sound that made his brain turn to mush. His chest tightened. She'd called his bluff in such a delightful way.

Setting down her glass, she folded her arms, and her expression sobered, but the ghost of a smile continued to tug at her lips. "Listen, Ron. I'm glad you came by. And not just for saving me from a choking attack. I wanted to talk to you...not that this is the best place, but our paths rarely cross elsewhere. I'm sorry I've been such a mess about whether to be friends...or more. If you can't already tell, I'm terrified for a lot of reasons, and I'm still not convinced starting a relationship in the middle of a war is the best idea, but I'd like to give it a try. That didn't sound too good, did it?" She sighed. "I'm rambling, aren't I? Believe it or not, I rehearsed what I wanted to say."

His breath whooshed out as if he'd been struck, and he gripped the table to keep from leaping up and grabbing her in an embrace that might squeeze the life from her. Doris cared about him. She didn't say the words, but her body language told him what he needed to know.

"Say something. Is it too late? Have you given up on me?" A frown creased her forehead.

"No. Frankly, I'm stunned…but in a good way." He allowed himself to reach for her hand, and she nestled her fingers in his, deepening the desire to draw her to him. "I've got news about the transfer I told you about. I hope you'll be as thrilled as I am."

Her face took on a guarded expression, and he gave himself a mental kick for his insensitivity. She must think he was leaving her behind.

"I'm taking the position at Frogmore Hospital, and you're going with me. While speaking with the regional director, I discovered the facility is short on mechanics and drivers. They recently lost four in some sort of accident giving us the perfect opportunity to explore our relationship."

She gaped at him, mouth moving but no sound coming out.

"Wait. That sounded too clinical." He squeezed her hand. "I want you to be my girl, and a fresh start at a new hospital might be the ticket."

"Are you asking me to go steady, Dr. McCann? If so, I accept, and the transfer sounds wonderful." A shy smile lit up her face, and she returned the pressure in his fingers.

"You've made me the happiest man on earth, Miss Strealer."

Her smile turned saucy. "You're welcome, Dr. McCann."

His guffaw split the air, and the group at the next table turned to stare for a brief moment. "You are a firecracker. The assignment starts on Monday, so we've got a few days to tie up our work here and do any turnover required." He rubbed his hands together.

"How did you get the transfer approved? Normally, new assignments aren't available until after six months."

"The director owed me a favor, and the new hospital is desperate for help. This place will only be down one until your replacement can be found, whereas Heritage Hall will still be down three even after you start. And by the way, one of the gals who was killed was the lead mechanic, so the transfer comes with a promotion."

She narrowed her eyes. "First the cook, and now the director. How many favors do you have left to call in?"

He wiggled his eyebrows. "I can't let you have all my secrets yet." He leaned the chair back and hoped the look he gave her was one of nonchalance. She had no idea how she affected him. He wanted to make her happy, to hear her silvery laugh, and to create a way for her to continue with her passion of working on cars. He wanted to be a better man, and no one, not even Phoebe, had ignited that desire in him. He'd never needed a woman before, not like this. His relationship with Phoebe had been shallow in comparison. She'd been his fiancée, but theirs had not been a deep, abiding relationship. Injured pride, not hurt, had been the result of her breaking off their engagement.

He would not fail this time. Doris deserved his utmost. Now, if he could only figure out how to be the best man he could.

Chapter Twenty-One

"That's the last of it." Doris shoved a heavy box into the back of the jeep then shielded her eyes against the glaring sun. Four o'clock, and the temperature was still in the eighties. The day had been a scorcher. "Did you bring every book you own?"

"No, but close. What about you? Your toolbox weighs a ton." Hands on his hips, Ron stood next to the driver's side of the vehicle.

"And I need everything in it." She smirked. "Do those books mean you haven't learned everything yet?"

"You are full of yourself this morning, aren't you?" He looked pleased with his repartee. "I'll drive for a change. You must get tired of driving."

She nodded. "I'd much rather work on vehicles than drive them, but that task comes with the territory. I can't make any promises about heckling you about your skills."

"I'm counting on your sass. It's one of the things I love about you."

Her breath caught. He'd said the word in jest, but was there a kernel of truth in his conversation? She was not ready for any declarations of love. Was he? "I have so many traits from which to choose." She climbed into the passenger seat and finger-combed her hair. Wearing a skirt and blouse instead of her coveralls felt good. Sometimes she tired of the bulky canvas uniform with its accompanying clunky shoes. "Let's get this show on the road."

He grinned. "Last week you weren't sure you wanted the new assignment; now you're raring to go."

"I'm using my woman's prerogative to change my mind." She wiggled her eyebrows and cocked her head. "Drive on, MacDuff."

"You are a pip." Shaking his head and wearing a wide grin, he slid behind the wheel and started the engine. "Okay, let the adventures begin." He drove down the tree-lined lane leading to the gate.

Birdsong sounded among the branches. Doris took a deep breath, trying to clear away the uncertainty and nerves of starting a new job. Insecurity nipped at her, and she wiped damp palms on her skirt.

Ron patted her shoulder. "Relax. You're going to be great. They'll love you, and no one will be more adept at the work than you. How about if we talk about our favorite things about being in England? You start."

The heaviness lifted from her chest. He was right. Well, maybe not about her new coworkers loving her, but she was good at her job, and that's what counted. "Hmmm. Okay. I like that I get to work on cars and trucks."

"Fair enough, but you need to try harder on the next one. Engine repair is your favorite activity no matter where you are. Now, me. My favorite thing is you being here."

Doris rolled her eyes, but warmth suffused her. "Too easy. Try again."

"How about the great food?"

"You must be eating somewhere besides the dining hall." She scoffed then gestured to the landscape. "How about this: the scenery is beautiful when it's not being bombed."

He cocked his head. "An interesting take on the situation."

Miles passed quickly as they regaled each other with what they enjoyed about being in England and memories of time at home. The sun began to dip, bringing relief from the searing heat. The jeep bumped over the uneven road surface, and she gripped the seat to keep from being hurled into Ron's lap or out the side.

"How many thousands of dollars will it take to bring this poor country back from destruction?"

"Untold amounts, for sure."

Distant buzzing sounded, and a chill swept over her. She glanced at Ron who'd stiffened and sat up straight. He met her gaze for a second then scanned the sky. The droning noise got louder, and he slowed the vehicle.

Her muscles trembled as she waited to see what sort of planes appeared overhead. Would their wings display the trio of concentric circles of the RAF emblem or the crooked black cross of the Germans? She held her breath and clenched her hands, fingernails biting into her palms.

Ron braked, and the jeep stopped, any pretense of nonchalance gone. He reached over and cradled her hands in his.

The buzz became a growl then a roar as the fleet approached. The lead aircraft appeared, and the dreaded whistle of falling bombs pierced the air. One by one, the planes dropped their load.

"Get out! We can't stay in the open." Ron shoved open his door and jumped out of the jeep.

Heart pounding, Doris tried to follow him, but her door was jammed. "Ron!"

He raced to her side, reached in, and lifted her over the door, arms around her waist. He set her down then grabbed her hand, tugging her toward the tree cover.

Legs pounding, she raced alongside him. Her pocketbook, slung around her neck, slapped her side with every step. *Dear God, please keep us safe.* She looked overhead at the silhouettes spewing shells from their bellies. Her stomach clenched, her breakfast threatening to reappear. The trite comment about the bombing seemed cavalier and insensitive in the face of reality.

The whistling intensified, and explosions rocked the earth behind them. Doris covered her ears and screamed. She stumbled and fell to one knee. Ron jerked her to her feet, nearly wrenching her arm from the socket. She winced at the pain but continued to run. What was a little pain when their lives hung in the balance?

Tears flood her eyes, and her vision blurred. She swiped away the moisture, her breath ragged.

Finally at the tree line, they dove into the underbrush. Ron crawled forward then pointed to a deep depression in the ground. "There. The hole may be our best bet." His voice was hoarse, and scratches marred his handsome face. "Can you make it?"

"Yes." Doris gritted her teeth and scuttled forward, spitting out dirt the forest floor tossed into her face. She rolled into the hole, and Ron followed her, shielding her with his body as he'd done the last time they'd been caught in a raid.

Kaboom!

The jeep exploded in a fireball. The deafening roar battered her ears. Soil and shrapnel rained down from above. Death had never seemed so close.

———————◆———————

Ron's heart thundered in his chest. Doris was curled into a tight ball underneath him, her body trembling in violent spasms. She was obviously terrified. He certainly was. No training in the world prepared someone to be subjected to aerial bombing. He whispered assurances into her ear that she might not hear because of the noise, but the action made him feel better, like he was actually doing something to alleviate her fear. Would their lives be snuffed out and his second chance with her obliterated?

The barrage lessened, becoming a muted rumble as the last few planes disappeared over the horizon. Soon all was quiet except for the crackling fire of the jeep that continued to burn, its oily, acrid smell drifting toward them on the breeze.

Lifting his head, he scanned the sky then their surroundings. Once again, they were alone and safe for the moment. He hugged Doris to himself. "Are you all right? Did you sustain any injuries?" He released her and helped her sit up then began to run his fingers lightly along her arms, his physician's training kicking in.

She shuddered and shook her head, eyes wide and brimming with tears. "I-I-I think I'm okay." She looked past him at the jeep and wrapped her arms around her middle. "That could have been us. We could have been killed. So close. Death is so close."

He thumbed the moisture off her face. "But it wasn't us. God kept us safe." Ron tucked her hair behind her ears then stroked her cheek. He lifted her chin until her gaze met his. "As uncomfortable as it will be, we should camp for the night. I'm not sure the exact distance, but we have at least fifteen miles to go, and I'm not prepared to walk that right now. By staying here, we have the shelter of the trees."

Relief swept over her face, and he knew he'd made the right decision. The dank earth seeped through the knees of his pants. "Are you okay to stand? I'd rather not spend the night in the hole."

"Yes." She gave him a resolute nod. "At least not until we line it with leaves or something to absorb the dampness. I'm a mess."

"You're the prettiest mess I've ever seen." He winked and grabbed her hand as she struggled to stand.

Her face reddened. "Probably not, but it's nice of you to say." She brushed dirt and debris from her clothes. "I was so happy not to be wearing my coveralls for the journey. They would have been a much better choice." She eyed the jeep again. The flames were dissipating, but smoke continued to engulf the vehicle. "Our belongings…everything…they're gone. Oh, Ron…all your books. I'm so sorry you lost your books."

"They're just things. I can replace them, but I can't replace you."

Chapter Twenty-Two

Doris climbed to her feet and approached the charred shell of the jeep. The vehicle had finally finished burning a short time after dark the previous evening. The blackened metal frames of their suitcases twisted and bent like some ghoulish sculpture. God had once again saved Ron and her from death. Did she have what it took to continue living this precarious life she'd chosen?

She glanced at Ron who stood a few yards away, hands stuffed in his pockets. Concern creased his forehead, and she gave him what she hoped was a reassuring smile. His face smoothed, and he nodded. She walked toward him, running her fingers through her hair in an effort to unsnarl the tangles. Was it a blessing or a curse that she didn't have a mirror to check her appearance?

"How do you feel?" Ron cocked his head. "That culvert wasn't exactly the Ritz-Carlton."

"Well enough. Surprisingly, I didn't suffer any nightmares, but sleep was a long time coming, and I woke often."

"Are you ready to set out?"

"And if I'm not?" She smirked and put her hands on her hips. "We could stay and wait for someone to drive by."

"We could, but who knows when that would happen. This isn't exactly a thoroughfare."

"I'm kidding." She held out her arms. "On the bright side, we should make good time because we're not burdened with carrying anything."

"But we should pace ourselves. Too much exertion will dehydrate us, and who knows when we'll come upon a pure water source. The temperature is already rising."

"Good point, Doctor. Always thinking ahead."

He looked pleased with her compliment.

Doris tugged at her blouse then smoothed her filthy skirt. She poked her pointer finger through a tear that had happened sometime during the mayhem. Fortunately, the split in the fabric was near the hem and not anywhere that would expose her undergarments. Although not as impractical as high-heeled pumps, her oxfords were not designed for hiking. Blisters were sure to form.

"Right. Best get to it, then." She gestured in the direction of their destination. "How about if you set our speed."

He began to walk, and she set her stride to match his. This was one time she was glad of her height. She wouldn't be scrambling to keep up with him. They walked in silence, and she was struck by the bird and animal activity in the trees lining the lane. As if the creatures knew the danger was gone, and it was safe to play and sing.

She tried to push the memory of the attack to the back of her mind, but the menacing sound of the engines and piercing scream of the bombs refused to go away. Her heart raced and her palms sweat. A deep sigh escaped. She pressed her lips together and studied the gravelly road under her feet.

Ron squeezed her shoulder. "I'm no psychologist, but you can talk to me about yesterday. I'm still shook up over the bombing. You must be also. Being subjected to air attacks isn't normal. Our brains and emotions have no point of reference to deal with the incident."

"You're so clinical. How do you do that?"

"No, I may sound analytical but I continue to relive the incident. Was there anything I could have done differently? What if I had died? Or worse, you." He flinched. "And as you can see, I've got muscle spasms. When will man stop killing one another?"

"I'd rather talk about anything but the raid. Eventually, I'll have to deal with the attack, but right now, out in the open, so soon afterward, I want to focus on the positive. We didn't die, and we're headed to two new positions we're going to enjoy. Or how about if we dream about what we'll be doing after the war. The tide is turning against the Axis, so the conflict can't last much longer, can it?"

"Probably longer than we realize or would prefer. But yes, I believe Hitler and his cronies will be overthrown." He shrugged. "I haven't given a lot of thought to what I'll do after I muster out. I was drafted almost the moment my residency ended."

"Do you have somewhere you'd like to live or a hospital you'd like to work?" She kicked at a stone, and it skittered across the broken macadam. Would he select a location far from their home?

"I want to be close to my family, not necessarily in the same place, but near enough to visit regularly. This war has taught me about the brevity of life, and I don't want to miss any chances to be with my folks and my sister, especially during important events like birthdays and holidays."

"There are lots of hospitals in Boston."

"Yes, but the city is too congested for my taste. Dartmouth has affiliations, and with my having graduated from there, perhaps I can get in with one of them." He frowned. "Although, patching up boys from the front and air-raid victims may not be the skill set they seek."

"Nonsense, any hospital would be lucky to have you. A traumatic injury is a traumatic injury, and the wherewithal to handle such a wound is a crucial skill to possess." Where had the self-assured, egotistical man gone? Would she ever get used to the new Ron?

"Kind of you to say, and I'm trying to leave my employment in God's hands, but I keep yanking it back."

Doris chuckled. "I have the same problem. One minute handing over my problems, and the next clutching the issue so tight that God has to pry it off my fingers." Doris chuckled, and the tightness in her chest eased. When she wasn't overthinking her relationship with Ron, she enjoyed their time together. He was smart and sensitive, nothing like when she'd arrived a few short months ago. Why did she get wrapped around the axle when it came to her feelings about him? She was allowing external circumstances to influence her internal thoughts. Buffeted by concern about what other people thought or situations she couldn't control. Which Bible verse talked about that? A bunch of them, no doubt.

She peeked at him from her peripheral vision.

He caught her glance and grinned, his face lighting up despite their predicament.

Her face warmed, and she looked at the ground. Imaginary squirrels danced in her stomach. Doris pressed her lips together. Such a schoolgirl reaction. No. Her feelings ran stronger than mere childish infatuation. She could no longer deny that she loved Ron.

But what she would do with that fact remained to be seen.

———————◆———————

Ron swallowed a smile. Had he ever met a more complex woman? Doris was a fascinating combination of brash confidence in her abilities as a mechanic, insecurity in her beauty as a woman, and dedication to her faith. He'd learned a lot from her since she'd arrived, and she'd given him much food for thought about his own relationship with His heavenly Father. A rather tenuous connection until recently if he were honest with himself. But thanks to Doris, he was on the right track to becoming a man of God.

Miles passed, and the sun rose higher, its humid heat creating a shimmer on the distant horizon. He'd lost track of how far they'd walked. A fair distance if his throbbing feet and burning calves were any indication.

He pulled out his handkerchief and wiped the sweat from his face then blotted his neck. "Would you like to take a break?"

"Not yet." She pointed to a bend several hundred yards away. "We'll stop at that curve and rest in the shade."

"Deal." He stuffed the damp hankie back into his pocket and squinted down the street. Movement in the meadow on the right caught his attention. Wildlife or domesticated animals? He cupped his hands around his eyes and peered at the distance shapes. Dozens of milling, wandering brown-and-white blobs.

Grabbing Doris's arm, he pointed toward the herd. "Cows. I think those are cows. And where there are farm animals, there are—"

"Farms. People." Doris grinned and wrapped her arms around him. "We're saved." She blushed and extricated herself. "Well…that might a bit of an overstatement."

"I don't think so. The last twenty-four hours have been difficult to say the least. We'll be able to report in and secure transportation from the hospital. Our trek is almost complete."

"The end is in sight."

He nodded. No need to put a damper on her celebration if the farm or its village wasn't just around the corner.

Doris hurried forward, and he stayed her with his hand. "Slow down, honey. If you tax all your strength now, you may not make the final leg."

"You're right. Of course. Silly of me."

"Not at all. I'm as thrilled as you that humanity isn't far, but my training makes me a wet blanket."

"Thanks for not making fun of me."

"Never."

She began to tug and pull at her clothes then rubbed at the dirt and grass stains.

He stroked her hair. "You're worried about first impressions. Don't be. We survived an aerial raid and a night in the woods. This village may have lost family and friends. Our appearance won't be of concern." He huffed out a sigh. "I'm not sure what I can do without my medical bag and the supplies we lost."

"God will provide a way."

"He will indeed. Thanks for the reminder." He winked. "We talked earlier about giving Him control. How soon I forget."

As they drew closer to the herd, the cows ambled toward the fence, mooing and grunting.

"I believe they're cheering us on." Ron executed an exaggerated bow. "Thank you, ladies. We appreciate your support."

Doris laughed and clapped her hands. "They're asking why we're taking so long to get where we're going."

"No, that's you."

They rounded the bend and stopped. Stretched on either side of the road were small homes, each surrounded by row after row of vegetable plants. Apparently the residents had turned every square inch of land into Victory gardens. Few people were in sight, and quiet enveloped the village.

Confusion on her face, Doris turned to him. "Where is everyone? We should have heard noise long before we arrived."

"I see no cars, so there are no engines roaring. It's midday, so perhaps the children are in school, and the mothers are inside or at work."

"Makes sense." She gestured to a stone building, larger than the rest, and a sign swinging in the breeze. "The White Stag. I'm famished. We can get a meal, and with any luck they have a telephone."

"Brilliant." He rubbed his hands together. "And perhaps they know where we can clean up."

As one, they hastened their steps and arrived at the front door to the pub moments later. Ron opened the door, and Doris slipped inside ahead of him.

After being outside in the bright sunlight, the internal dimness seemed gloomy and suffocating. His eyes gradually adjusted, but with few windows and even fewer lightbulbs in use, the room remained dismal. He approached the counter where the elderly barkeep polished the wood as if his life depended on it. Ron smiled. "Good afternoon, sir. We lost our jeep yesterday in a bombing raid. Do you have a telephone we might use to contact my hospital?"

"Land sakes, an American."

"Two, actually." Doris raised her hand.

"Well, missy. Where did you come from?" The man's bright black eyes and cocked head made him resemble a curious finch. "Wait. Don't tell me. You're one of them USO folks going to entertain the troops."

She shook her head. "No, and if you heard me sing, you'd know why I'm a Red Cross gal."

He chortled, and his gaze swung to Ron. "Are you a Red Cross lad?"

"No. I'm a physician with the Army Medical Corps. We've been transferred to Frogmore Hospital." Ron leaned on the bar. "I didn't see any bomb damage. Did the Jerries miss your village?"

"By a mile or so. Old Mr. Wellington has a crater in his back field, but other than that, we're snug as a bug as they say. I'm sorry to hear about your vehicle. Are there only two of you?"

"Yes. We didn't lose anyone in the raid."

"Good news, to be sure. Life's perilous these days." He gestured to a nearby table. "Have a seat, and the missus will be right out with tonight's dinner. We don't offer a menu anymore. We serve what we've got."

"I'm sure the food will be delicious." Doris laid her hand on the man's arm. "Is there somewhere I may freshen up?"

"Yes, up the stairs. First room on the right. Take all the time you need, and there are clothes in the cabinet free for the taking."

"Thank you, sir."

"Now, we'll have none of that. The name's Gavin."

Doris beamed. "Gavin. And I'm Doris." She squeezed Ron's arm then traipsed up the stairs, footsteps light on the treads.

"She's a pretty one." The man tossed his rag in the sink. "Special, is she? You watch her like she means something to you."

Ron slid onto the stool. "She does." Words poured out as he recounted the weeks since Doris had arrived. What was it about the man that created the desire to share their story?

"Have you told her you love her?"

"It's complicated."

A throat cleared behind him, and he turned. Doris stood behind him, face set in stone. How much had she heard?

Chapter Twenty-Three

Doris studied Ron's red face. He looked guilty, but she'd failed to hear his discussion with the barkeep. Would she be able to finagle their conversation from him? No. She needed to stop looking for intrigue and machinations with regard to Ron. Sliding onto to the stool next to him, she smiled. "Thanks for the use of the room and the clothes. I feel less bedraggled and a whole lot more clean." She nudged Ron's shoulder and wrinkled her nose. "You might consider a trip upstairs."

A petite woman whose gray hair peeked out from under a kerchief appeared balancing two steaming bowls and a platter of bread on her arms.

"Later." His stomach rumbled. "Lunch first."

"Welcome." The woman set the dishes on the counter with a thump. "I'm Marie. There's more where that came from."

"Thank you, Marie." Doris inhaled the fragrant concoction. "Chicken stew? Smells divine."

Marie beamed. "A family recipe that's been passed down for generations. Enjoy." She tugged on Gavin's arm. "Give the young people some privacy, Gavin. You've got plenty of chores to amuse you."

Gavin bowed. "Yes, ma'am. Your wish is my command. I'll get to them straightaway."

"Ma'am. Pish posh. I'm not the queen." She winked at Doris and hurried to the kitchen, Gavin close on her heels.

"We see who runs the joint, eh?" Ron pointed at the swinging door with his spoon. "Guess I best get used to the idea. I heard there's a female doctor at the hospital. Since Roosevelt let women into the Army and Navy Medical Corps, enlistment has been up."

"You're trying to agitate me, aren't you? It won't work. I know you've left your caveman ways behind."

Ron chuckled. "Thought I'd get you going but no luck. By the way, I telephoned the hospital, and they're sending a jeep." He glanced at his watch. "Should be here in fifteen minutes, maybe sooner. The idea of riding the remaining ten miles to the hospital makes me giddy."

"Giddy? Not an emotion I've seen from you yet."

"Then you should enjoy the show." He finished his stew and sopped up the remaining gravy with some bread. He pushed away the plate and patted his stomach. "I'm stuffed. I'll go clean up. Shouldn't be long. Don't want to miss my ride."

"Afraid I'll make you walk?"

"You wouldn't dare." He gave her a sly smile and hurried toward the steps.

She sighed and ate her remaining stew, savoring in the food's zesty taste. Home cooking as good as her mom's. Her heart tugged. Mom and Dad would be sitting down to dinner shortly. Every day that passed, she rearranged her things-to-do-as-soon-as-I-get-home list, but near the top was a family meal.

Gavin returned to retrieve the soiled dishes. "The food was to your liking, then?"

"Fantastic. Brought to mind my mom's cooking." She wiped her mouth on the napkin and laid it on the counter. "You wouldn't want to tell me what you and Ron were discussing when I came downstairs, would you?"

"That'd be the lad to say, not me. But I'll be praying for the two of you."

"Uh…thanks." What had they talked about? She slid off the stool. "Let Ron know I'll wait for him outside."

"Sure. Safe road, missy."

Doris pulled at the ill-fitting slacks and blouse, the only items in the bureau close to her size. What would the hospital director say to her showing up wearing pants? Hopefully, he'd be glad she made it to his facility alive. She pushed open the door and stepped into the sunlight. A light breeze stroked her cheek, and she let out a sigh. Count your blessings, Doris, and stop worrying. A skylark warbled overhead, chiming in with his agreement. *Thank You for the reminder, Father. Forgive my unbelief.*

The door opened behind her, and Ron appeared as a jeep braked in front of the pub. The driver, a muscular corporal sporting a blond crew cut, lifted his hand in greeting. "Are you Dr. McCann and Miss Strealer?"

Doris nodded.

"I'm Corporal Nickels. Hop in, and I'll have you back in a jiffy. Word is you folks had a narrow miss yesterday. Glad you made it."

Ron helped Doris into the jeep, his hands sending tingles up her arms. She settled into the seat while he stepped onto the wheel and crawled into the back. "Ready, Corporal."

The vehicle lurched forward, and the corporal kept up a steady one-sided conversation as they bumped and shimmied along the road. A plane rumbled in the cloudless sky, and Doris flinched. Sweat sprang out on her palms, and her gaze shot toward the craft. The concentric circles of the RAF were emblazoned on the wings, and her breath hitched. Not the enemy. She blinked back tears of relief and wiped her hands on the coarse, borrowed slacks.

A hand squeezed her shoulder, and she turned. Ron gave her a reassuring smile but didn't say anything.

Peace flooded her, and she returned his smile. A few minutes later, they arrived at the hospital, climbed out of the jeep, and went inside. Controlled chaos seemed to reign. White-coated doctors, uniformed Red Cross nurses, and orderlies conversed in quiet tones as they strode through the lobby.

Doris gestured to the large wooden desk at the back of the room.

The young woman held up her hand as she spoke into a telephone receiver. Hanging up, she studied them with pursed lips. "Dr. McCann? Miss Strealer?"

"Yes."

"Director Braverman will see you now. You may leave your luggage with me."

"We don't have any bags." Doris shrugged. "Our personal effects were lost when our jeep was bombed."

"Oh, dear. Well, that certainly explains your outfit." She jerked her head to a door on her left. "Through there."

Ron frowned. Doris's red face and stiff posture trumpeted her embarrassment. The woman's rudeness knew no bounds. Time to put her in her place. "Yes, it's unfortunate that we managed to escape with our lives but not our luggage. Please accept our apologies for our fashion faux pas."

The receptionist's face flamed. "Uh—"

"No need to respond. We've got an appointment to keep." He tucked Doris's hand into the crook of his elbow. "Chin up, honey. Even in sackcloth, you're prettier than any other woman."

A tremulous smile tugged at Doris's mouth, and she squeezed his arm. "Thank you. I—"

He put his index finger to his lips. "Shh. I meant every word, and the woman should be formally reprimanded, but I don't want to make waves on my first day."

"Your words held enough sting. We should show her some grace. Perhaps she doesn't know the Lord."

Ron sighed. A chance to be a witness for God, and he'd blown the opportunity. "Well said."

They followed the woman's directions and were soon in front of the director's office. Ron knocked once then opened the door so they could step inside.

Sparsely furnished with worn-out government-issue furniture, the room was about ten feet square. A framed photo of Roosevelt hung behind the gray-haired man who sat at the scarred wooden desk. Stacks of paper covered most of the desk's surface. The remnants of a sandwich lay on a chipped plate at his elbow. He continued to scribble on a piece of paper, the scratching of his fountain pen the only sound in the room.

Doris withdrew her hand from Ron's arm and laced her fingers. A muscle jumped in her jaw, and he longed to stroke the tension from her face. He settled for what he hoped was a reassuring smile. He turned back to toward the director and stood at attention, barely breathing. Was the man's delay a power play or was he truly overwhelmed with the sea of paperwork on his desk?

After interminable minutes, Director Braverman laid down his pen and looked up at them, his gaze unwavering. Behind his black horn-rimmed spectacles, his gray eyes were steely, matching his stoic face. He removed his glasses and tossed them on the pile of paper in front of him. "You were supposed to arrive yesterday. We were inundated with casualties from a bombing raid and could have used you. What sort of excuse do you have for your tardiness?"

Ron rocked back on his heels at the acid in the man's tone. "Sir, we were caught in the same raid. Our jeep was destroyed. Did you not receive our message? We telephoned this morning, and a vehicle was sent to fetch us. Was that directive not from you?"

"I'm aware of your difficulties. What I want to know is why you didn't arrive sooner."

"Sir—"

Director Braverman's piercing glare swung to Doris. "I was speaking to Dr. McCann, Miss Strealer. You'll refrain from talking unless I indicate otherwise. Is that clear?"

Her face blanched. "Yes, sir."

Ron's stomach clenched, and he gritted his teeth. No wonder the receptionist was snippy. This guy was a dragon. "I felt it was safer to hole up for the night rather than hike in the darkness; therefore, we remained at our location and set out at first light. Without water or sustenance, we were unable to make good time, so we didn't arrive in the village until midday. We reported in upon our arrival."

The man's eyes narrowed. "Protocol is that you make contact as soon as practicable, yet you chose to delay your journey until daybreak. Are you a coward, man?"

"What? No." Ron's nostrils flared. "I analyzed the situation and felt the best course of action was to wait."

"So your course of action was no action." Director Braverman frowned. "Do you realize your choice has put a stain on the reputation of the Red Cross and the U.S. Army Medical Corps? Do you care nothing about your own reputations?" He sat back and crossed his arms. "You have been compromised."

"In what way, sir?" Ron's chest tightened, and he stuffed his hands into his pockets so the condescending man couldn't see his fists. "I don't understand your reaction. We are bombing victims, yet we are being treated like perpetrators of a crime."

"Your behavior is a crime. You and this young woman were alone, in the woods, at night. Who's to say what happened between the two of you."

Doris gasped then clapped a hand over her mouth.

Ron straightened his spine and rose to his full height. How dare the man insinuate he and Doris had been intimate. He took a deep breath. "Sir, I resent the implication that anything untoward happened between Miss Strealer and me. My medical opinion of her well-being was that a night of rest was required before striking out on a twenty-mile hike. You and anyone else who assume we were inappropriate is making a mistake, and I don't appreciate it. Her behavior was above reproach as was mine. We are professionals reporting for duty and would like to be dismissed so we can get to work." He fought the urge to sneer. "After all, you were deluged with patients. I'm sure my skills can be put to use."

"Quite a speech, McCann. A trifle insubordinate, if you ask me. I've a mind to make a report about the incident and your current disrespect. I have only your word about the situation, but Miss Strealer's reputation precedes her. This isn't the first time she's found herself in a ticklish position."

"What are you talking about?" Red faced, Doris stalked to the desk.

Ron mentally cheered her on, glad to see she wasn't going to cower under the man's snide accusations.

"Early in your most recent assignment, there was an occurrence of inappropriate behavior at a local pub. You accosted one of our soldiers and made certain suggestions about possible activities. The young man was, of course, offended and turned her down. Personally, I'm disappointed the Red Cross let you continue in its ranks. To have such a loose woman in their employ doesn't seem right."

"Who has made these false claims? Nothing of the sort happened," Doris sputtered, fisted hands on her hips. Realization seemed to dawn on her face, and she scowled. "Wait. There was that guy. That terrible man who made lewd comments to me. He manhandled me, and I stomped on his foot. He tried to hit me, but Ron…Dr. McCann intervened." Venom dripped from her words. "If you want to file a report, I'd be happy to make one against him."

"A little late now, don't you think? Seems like you want to take the attention off yourself."

Ron's heart thudded against his chest. Had he made a poor choice in staying in the woods? Had he besmirched Doris's reputation? What could he do to make things right?

He stepped forward. "Sir, I protest this line of questioning. We have made our statements. If you choose not to believe us, I will go up the chain of command to get the matter straightened out. To Chairman Davis, if necessary, or...Mrs. Roosevelt."

Chapter Twenty-Four

Doris stared at Ron, jaw agape. His offer to go over the director's head punched a hole in her anger. Would he really escalate the misunderstanding to the White House? Surely not. But it meant a lot that he would consider going to the president's wife or at least threaten to do so. Making a big deal out of the situation would only create additional problems. If Director Braverman were telling the truth, and her reputation was in tatters, she should lay low, not attract the attention of the newspapers. Anything associated with Mrs. Roosevelt was newsworthy, especially the efforts she made on behalf of women.

The man sat behind the desk, fingers steepled and placed under his chin, a smug smile on his face. He almost seemed triumphant that he'd ferreted out the so-called situation.

She rubbed her throbbing forehead. "Why will you not believe us, Director Braverman? You're taking the word of one man without doing any sort of investigation. Have you spoken with my supervisor or my colleagues? How about people who were at the pub that evening? I deserve an opportunity to clear my name."

He rose. "How do you know that I've not done my homework?"

Heart pounding, Doris licked her lips. "Because you would have discovered the man is lying, and that I'm not the kind of woman you seem to think I am."

"Look, sweetheart—"

"Sweetheart—"

Holding up his hand, he shook his head. "It's enough that we have the nurses here, but women don't belong in a war zone, especially in the motor corps. So, you didn't do what he said, but you were out all night with Dr. McCann, which doesn't look good. I won't have a black mark on the name of this hospital."

"You can't fire me."

"But I can tell the Red Cross I don't want you for the reasons we've discussed. They can take care of letting you go."

"Fine. I'll resign. Will that make you happy?" Her lips trembled, and she pressed them together. She couldn't let this despicable man know how he affected her. He obviously considered women beneath him. A crying woman would only confirm his opinion.

He shrugged. "Wonderful. Takes the problem off my desk."

"You unfeeling jerk." Ron growled. "How did the army let you get into a position of leadership?"

"Careful, McCann. I don't want to have to bring you up on charges."

Doris laid her hand on his arm, his warmth sending tingles through her palm. Her skin tingled as she silently pled him to rein in his temper.

Shouting at the director wouldn't solve the problem. In fact, the conversation couldn't get much worse. If she went away quietly, Ron's reputation had a chance to recover, and with any luck, the lies about her behavior wouldn't follow her.

How had her life turned from joyful and exciting to dismal in an instant? Being wrongly accused wasn't fair. If she couldn't find another organization to take her, she'd return home in disgrace. And to add insult to injury, she'd have to pay her own way. The Red Cross certainly wouldn't pay her fare once they heard the lies or she resigned.

I'm with you, My child. All will be well.

She blinked and looked at Ron. He was still glaring at Director Braverman, so he'd not heard the voice. Jesus himself had been falsely accused. She shouldn't expect different treatment. Pride and sorrow warred with the peace that was trying to wrap itself around her heart. She'd find somewhere to stay then pray long and hard about what to do next. The situation was in God's hands, so the outcome would be for His glory. The lack of control was a hard pill to swallow, but she'd been operating on her own for too long. Time to nestle close to her heavenly Father.

Ron would get over her, and with lots of time, perhaps she might be able to forget him.

"We could get married." Ron blurted out the words in the deafening silence that had blanketed the room since he'd started his staring contest with the director.

"What?"

"What?"

He glanced between Doris and Director Braverman. Both gaped at him, eyes wide, and faces etched in shock. Before he could change his mind, he dropped to one knee and took Doris's hands in his. "This isn't how I planned to ask you, but will you marry me? You'd make me the happiest man on earth if you'll say yes."

He held his breath as myriad emotions fought for supremacy on her face. Uncertainty, anxiety, disappointment, and another emotion he couldn't read, played across her expression.

Finally, when he could stand it no longer, she squeezed his fingers and shook her head. "No. I'm sorry, Ron. I can't marry you." A single tear trickled down her cheek, and she swiped it away. "I'm sorry." Barely above a whisper, her voice battered his ears as if she'd shouted her answer.

"I'm sorry, too, Doris. I thought you had feelings for me." His heart shattered, and he staggered to his feet. He'd pick up the pieces later and lock them in a box so that no woman could ever have access. "But I will pursue this matter on your behalf if you'd like." His own voice sounded mechanical, no...clinical, as it should be.

"No, I'll submit my resignation and prayerfully consider my options. I'm doing this for you, Ron. We can't get married because of misplaced appearances or because it seems that we *have* to wed."

"But that's not why I'm asking."

"Yes, it is. You said it yourself. This isn't how you planned to ask me, yet you did." She leaned forward and kissed his cheek, a brief touch, almost as if butterfly wings had brushed his skin. "Someday you'll see this is for the best. Or if you still care after this awful war is over, you can look me up. Come see me, and if your feelings are still as you say…well, we'll see."

"But—"

She pressed her fingers to his lips. "Not another word. I'll be praying for you. I hope you'll do the same for me." She marched to the door and grabbed the handle. Without turning, she said, "And I'll be praying for you too, Director Braverman." She turned the knob and slipped into the hallway, closing the door with a soft *snick.*

Ron whirled toward the director, who'd remained silent through the entire exchange with Doris. His face held a mixture of awe and confusion. He met Ron's eyes and dropped into his seat. Picking up his pen, he grabbed a sheet of paper and began to write. "You're dismissed, Dr. McCann. I consider this matter closed, so let's hear no more about it. Miss Kernigan, the receptionist, will give you information about your lodging. Report to the second floor, and one of the nurses can familiarize you with the shift schedule and give you a tour. You'll shadow Dr. Leland for the first half of the night shift, then you'll be off duty until oh-seven-hundred tomorrow. Clear?"

"Crystal." Ron didn't bother with a salute. He strode out of the office. Doris's voice in his head cautioned him against slamming the door, so he left it open, unsure of his ability to tamp down his anger at the injustice he'd witnessed.

He gaze whipped back and forth in the corridor, then over the railing and into the foyer. No sign of Doris. She'd wasted no time in vacating the building. Where had she gone? Should he search for her? Why did she reject him? Had he really misread her feelings?

With heavy feet, he trudged downstairs to begin his new assignment, one that no longer held the enticement it did mere hours ago.

An officer in dress uniform trotted up the stairs toward him. The soldier seemed familiar. Where had he seen him? Perhaps he resembled someone in his past.

Then the man smiled, an oily smirk that took Ron back to the night he rescued Doris. Lieutenant Halifax. Stationed here.

God, keep me from punching this guy in the nose.

Chapter Twenty-Five

Doris slung her satchel over her shoulder and trudged through the gate at the 1st General Hospital compound. After fleeing Frogmore Hospital, she'd walked the streets for hours praying and considering her options. Exhausted and physically spent, she knew how Jacob of the Old Testament felt after wrestling with God. The Lord hadn't dislocated her hip, but her muscles ached as if she'd stacked ten cords of wood. Stomach growling with hunger, she found shelter in a small church that gave her a plain but filling dinner and a place to sleep. Most of the inhabitants had been displaced by bombs, their vacant, staring eyes indicative of the shock that still enveloped them.

The morning dawned fair and bright, so she gave the priest a few of her coins as a thank you then used the last of her money and ration stamps to purchase a couple of outfits and some toiletries. Without enough money to pick up new shoes, she was stuck with her scuffed oxfords that had seen better days. Perhaps a trip to the cobbler was in order, and she could get the soles replaced. She frowned. The repair might not be necessary if she was sent home.

She took a deep breath and surveyed the endless rows of buildings. Corrugated metal roofs covered the walkways that connected the structures. Electrical and telephone wires were strung on a line of poles that stretched farther than she could see. How many hundreds of servicemen could the facility hold? Too many to count probably.

A square brick edifice with several jeeps parked out front stood to the right of the gate. Above the double doors hung a sign: All Visitors Must Check In Here. Doris licked her lips and patted her hair, finally clean and tangle-free. She shook her head to clear the memory of the bombing and subsequent hike, but an image of Ron's face refused to leave. How long before he no longer clung to her heart like an insect to a windshield?

"Enough dillydallying, girl. Get this over and done with, then you can move on to the next chapter of your life." Doris smoothed her skirt and marched through the entrance. A blonde woman about her age sat behind the desk. She looked up as Doris entered and smiled. "Welcome. How may I help you?"

"I'm with the Red Cross Motor Corps, and I…uh…need to see whomever is in charge here. I realize I haven't made an appointment, but I'm willing to wait as long as necessary."

Footsteps sounded, and a short, buxom woman with dark hair hurried into the lobby.

The receptionist raised her hand. "Oh, there she is now. Mrs. Wilkinson, this gal needs to see you. She's from…." She turned to Doris, a quizzical expression on her face.

Doris stepped toward Mrs. Wilkinson, hand outstretched. "I'm Doris Strealer, recently of Heritage Hall Hospital. I need to discuss a delicate matter. That is, if you're available. I apologize for not telephoning before arriving."

Mrs. Wilkinson shook Doris's hand. "No worries, dearie. Life moves fast here. Appointments often fall by the wayside. I'm free at the moment, so let's step into my office." She glanced at the receptionist. "Pearl, be a love and bring us some tea and sandwiches."

"Yes, ma'am."

"Right this way." She led Doris into a tiny room with a table surrounded by chairs. Bookshelves and filing cabinets lined the walls. Stacks of paper covered most of the surfaces. "Please pardon the mess. I recently lost my assistant, and her replacement hasn't arrived yet. The poor woman may be sorry when she sees what she's gotten herself into, eh?" Mrs. Wilkinson laughed, a braying sound that reminded Doris of the mule on her grandfather's farm. The woman gestured to the vacant chairs and lowered her girth onto the closest one that creaked in protest.

Doris sat and clutched her satchel on her lap. "Thank you for seeing me, ma'am."

"Relax, dearie. Put your bag on the floor. We'll have a chin-wag, as the Brits like to say, until the food arrives, then after we've eaten, we'll address your situation. Serious discussions are best had on a full stomach, wouldn't you agree?"

"Uh…sure."

"Now, tell me all about yourself while we wait for Pearl. Where are you from, and why did you select the Red Cross as your way to serve our boys?"

"A village in New Hampshire near the mountains." A wave of homesickness swept over Doris. Would she live to see the wooded peaks of the White Mountains? She blinked and swallowed the lump that had formed in her throat then continued to give the kind woman her background information.

Partway through Doris's monologue, Pearl tiptoed in carrying a tray that held a teapot, two teacups, and a plate piled with sandwiches that she set on the table. Doris began to salivate, and her stomach gurgled.

Mrs. Wilkinson grinned. "Excellent. I like to see girls with a healthy appetite. Eat up."

Twenty minutes later, fully sated, Doris sighed and folded her hands. "Thank you. I didn't realize how hungry I was until the food arrived. You've been most generous with your supplies and your time."

"I must be honest, dearie, you had a haunted look in your eyes when you arrived and now not as much. My mama taught me to feed the body then the soul. We've done the first, now it's time for the second." She patted Doris's arm. "Tell me everything, then we'll take it to the Lord."

Doris startled. "You're a believer?"

"Yes, and it seems you are, too."

"Yes, ma'am, but I'm struggling to hold on to my faith. These last few days have been terrible." She outlined the events, beginning with the incident when she first saw Ron. Words poured out and occasional tears, but she soldiered on.

Mrs. Wilkinson remained mute except for a periodic sigh or encouraging murmur.

Drained yet filled with inexplicable peace, Doris fell silent. This must be what it felt like to share a burden, something she'd never been comfortable doing.

"Well, that is quite a story, but nothing that happens to us is too big for our heavenly Father. He knew about this situation before it occurred, and He knows about your future. So, let's go to Him and ask for wisdom, okay?"

Doris nodded. She reached for Mrs. Wilkinson's hands and clung to her fingers as if they were a lifeline.

"Dear Father God, thank You for bringing Doris to me. She is Your child and seeks to do Your will. She is wounded, hurting, and feeling beat up. Unjustly accused, she is at a loss about what to do. The world would suggest a response of vengeance, but we know vengeance only comes from You. It is not our place to exact revenge or paybacks. Please give us Your plan for her, and wrap her in Your loving arms. In Jesus' name, amen."

"Amen." Doris released Mrs. Wilkinson's hands and slumped in the chair. "Thank you. I feel a glimmer of hope."

"Excellent." Mrs. Wilkinson beamed then sobered up. "We have limited options, dearie, but I believe we can find a solution that suits. If you are willing to fight the allegations, you should consider seeking the assistance of an attorney, but the culprit is in the armed forces and may receive a lot of sympathy. He also may ship out soon if he hasn't already, so he'll be beyond your reach. If you'd like to put the incident behind you and start fresh, I can make some recommendations for organizations who need willing workers. You can choose one that doesn't cater to servicemen." She cocked her head. "Not that I don't want you to remain in the Red Cross, but I would imagine you might like to distance yourself from us."

"The temptation is to bring this man up on charges, but I don't believe that is what God would have me do. Instead, I will try to pray for him to see the error of his ways."

"Your decision shows your maturity and your willingness to show others the mercy God has bestowed to you. Do you want to continue serving in England? Do you want to continue working on vehicles or try another avenue?"

"I'm more comfortable with engines than people, Mrs. Wilkinson. Is there someone in London or the outskirts who can use a war-weary grease monkey?"

"I've got just the ticket."

Chapter Twenty-Six

Sweat trickled between Doris's shoulder blades as she reached farther into the engine compartment of the black sedan that had been converted to a staff car for one of the higher-ups. The vehicle had seen better days, and it was her responsibility to bring it back to life. She'd already replaced over half the parts and wasn't close to being finished. Some people might complain about the job. To her, the work was pure heaven. Just her and the hulking metal beast.

Mrs. Wilkinson had come through and secured her a position with the Mechanized Transport Corps, a British civilian organization for women. Founded in 1939 by one of the country's well-to-do women, the MTC originally provided its own vehicles and uniforms, but then the Ministry of War Transport got involved. Doris shrugged. As long she was able to work on vehicles in peace and quiet, she didn't care who ran the place. A week had passed since joining, and she still relished the ratio of a dozen women to one man which mean she didn't have to worry about romantic entanglements.

Because of her vast experience with cars and her time with the Red Cross, she was allowed to skip through most of the required recruit training that would have taken three weeks. Instead, she'd tested out of everything but the administration portion, so she spent an hour each afternoon in one of the parlor-turned-lecture halls. The twice-daily drills also cut into her work time, but with no other commitments, she made up time by often working into the evening.

Pockets of MTC squads were scattered all over England. Hers was located on a requisitioned country estate in the northwest suburbs of London, a gorgeous property that stretched for a square mile and consisted of a brick Georgian home that held administrative offices and ancient, well-maintained stone cottages that housed the staff. Four to a room was tight, but her three British roommates had accepted her with warm friendliness, never once questioning why she'd left the Red Cross or chosen the MTC.

Last night, they dragged her into town to one of the pubs and told everyone inside it was her birthday. When she protested that she wouldn't turn twenty-nine for another five months, Lucy claimed the war would be over by then, and they wouldn't have the chance to celebrate. Eva and Janet concurred and kept the ruse going all night, which resulted in free food and drink from several of the other patrons. She'd hastened to set the record straight with each delivery, but no one seemed to mind it wasn't her real birthday.

Doris shook her head and smiled. The silliness felt good after the difficulties and near-death experiences during the last few weeks. They were a good group of gals, and she was already closer to them than any of her so-called friends at home.

With a grunt, she tried to turn the wrench on the bolt that held the fuel pump in place. The stubborn metal spike wouldn't budge, so she grasped the tool with two hands and pulled with all her might. The bolt gave way and rotated with a screech. "You've met your match, sister." She removed the remaining fasteners and detached the tired-looking part. Hopefully, a good cleaning and some fresh gaskets would prevent the need to replace the piece. Tough to come by, she only had two new ones in stock.

The garage vibrated. Wrench in hand, she looked up as an ambulance rolled in behind her sedan, engine hiccupping. A tall, sandy-haired man got out and peered at her. Her heart skipped a beat. Would every ash-blond man remind her of Ron?

"May I help you?" She tucked the tool into the pocket of her coveralls.

His white armband emblazoned with a red cross was stark against his rumpled, green uniform. Smudges of dirt marked his tired, angular face. Piercing black eyes stared at her. His mouth was a slash above his square jaw, dark with two days growth of whiskers. "My ambulance needs a look. On my last trip, I could barely get any power out of her, and in the last few miles she started sounding like a drunken infantryman." He patted the vehicle. "I've heard you're the best."

Her eyes widened. "How could you know that? I just got here."

He shook his head. "Not you personally, the gals at this MTC squad. Can you fix her? I'm due back at eighteen hundred hours."

Face warm, she shrugged. "I'll have to get permission from my sergeant to bump you in front of this job, and until I inspect the vehicle, I won't know how long the repair will take. Perhaps you can find another ambulance."

"Not a chance, luv." He snapped his fingers. "Get cracking; I'm in a hurry."

She raised her eyebrow. His rudeness was unnecessary, and she was not going to allow herself to be bullied into action by some man. "How about if you get cracking? I'm busy." She pointed toward the small outbuilding two hundred yards away. "You can find Captain Derringer in there. Tell her I want the order in writing."

His face pinked under his tan. "You're a feisty one, luv, and I deserve your scorn. I apologize for my behavior. Twenty-four hours of trips transporting wounded from the Portsmouth to London has got me knackered. I'm not at my best."

"Understandable." She forced a smile. "Let's do this: you head to the dining hall for a cup of tea and something to eat, and I'll talk to the captain and get permission to work on your vehicle. I'll see if I can grab one of the other gals, so we can get this fixed toot sweet."

He blew out a deep breath. "Thank you. My friend is right. You are the best. By the way, I'm Corporal Pritchett."

"Nice to meet you, Corporal. I'm Corporal Strealer."

He held two fingers to his forehead in a quick salute then pivoted on his heels and hurried from the building.

"Well, that was interesting." She laid the pump on the nearby bench and wiped her hands on a rag, then walked to the telephone mounted on the wall and lifted the receiver. "Dolly, can you connect me to garage number two?" If the guy hadn't been so disrespectful, she'd have offered to call immediately, rather than telling him to go in person. She needed to get a handle on her temper. Her disappointment at Ron and anger at Director Braverman was coloring every interaction she had with the male of the species.

Minutes later, she hung up the phone having garnered permission to fix the guy's car with Lucy's help. He'd be happy, and so was she. The sooner she got the handsome medic on his way, the better.

Humming "Chattanooga Choo Choo," Doris danced across the cement floor to the ambulance. She popped the hood and began a methodic inspection of each part inside. The engine compartment was filthy as if the vehicle had driven through miles of mud puddles. No wonder the poor thing finally gasped in protest.

Footsteps.

Lucy or the cranky medic?

"The cavalry has arrived." Lucy pursed her lips and made a trumpet sound. "Have you diagnosed the problem yet?"

"No, but a good cleaning might be a good start."

Lucy peered over Doris's shoulder. "Wow. Where in the world was this guy driving?"

"He claims he was making runs from Portsmouth to London. Are the roads that bad?"

"I have no idea, but our job is to get this thing running again, not speculate about the guy's story. By the way, I passed him on the way here, and he's a looker, isn't he? Wonder why he's a medic and not a soldier? Must be something wrong with him."

Doris swatted Lucy's shoulder. "Focus."

"We don't get enough guys through here, and few have been as gorgeous. You've got to be blind not to see that."

"I admit he's cute, but standing around jawing won't get the job done, and he's in a rush. If we take too long, he may start trying to help, and the last thing I need is some guy breathing down my neck while I'm working." What would it be like to have him stand that close? Doris's face heated, and she ducked her head. Good grief. Now who wasn't focused?

"You're blushing. Maybe I should work on the ambulance, and you go keep him company in the dining hall."

"No!" The exclamation came out with more vehemence than she intended. "No. Look, I agree that he's nice looking, but I'm not in the market for a boyfriend. You are welcome to him." She slid behind the driver's seat and turned on the vehicle. Eyeing the gauges, she pressed her lips together. Oil pressure was almost nonexistent. She climbed out of the car then glanced at Lucy who stood with her arms crossed. "What?"

"You. That's what. Any girl in her right mind would be attracted to this guy. How come you're not?"

Doris blew out a loud breath. "I'm…uh…taking a break from dating."

"You've been hurt." Lucy cocked her head. "Recently?"

Unable to speak, Doris nodded.

"Oh, honey. I'm sorry. I wouldn't have ribbed you. That why you transferred?"

"Partly. The situation is complicated, but suffice it to say, my heart is beat up, and I'm not interested in making the mistake of getting close to any man ever again. Not all guys are untrustworthy, but apparently I'm not good at figuring out which ones are, so no thanks."

"You can't let one guy turn you inside out like that."

"It wasn't intentional."

"He didn't mean to hurt you?" Confusion flitted across Lucy's face. "Then you should give him a second chance."

"Maybe after the war. Right now I've got a job to do, and I'm not going to let anything, or anyone, interfere." If only she could convince her heart. "Now, let's get this baby back on the road. I think there's a problem with the lubricating system.

Lucy smirked and saluted. "Aye, aye."

"You're a regular riot."

"Doris?"

Doris whirled toward the voice. "Emily?"

Her younger sister stood in the doorway, wringing her hands.

"Emily, what's wrong? How did you find me?"

Chapter Twenty-Seven

Ron yanked off the cotton mask that covered his nose and mouth and dropped it in the bin by his feet. He rotated his shoulders to unkink the muscles, but after sixteen hours of surgery, his body would need serious time in bed to unwind. Unfortunately, every time he closed his eyes, images of Doris and their time together plagued him, making sleep impossible.

The nurse who'd been assisting him untied the string that held the gown over his clothes. He slipped his arms from the sleeves, and she tossed the garment on the gurney, then rolled everything in a ball before shoving the wad into the laundry bag. Another nurse wheeled the instrument tray out of the room, and a pair orderlies walked in carrying cleaning supplies. Their wide-eyed stares spoke of their wonder that he was still in the surgical theater.

"Sorry." He raked his fingers through his hair. "I'll let you get on with it." The last thing the staff needed was him in their way while doing their job. He marched out the swinging door and stopped. Now what. Too keyed up to head to his quarters and too dark to go for a stroll on the grounds. Perhaps some rounds would do him good.

He strode to the nurses' station.

The uniformed woman seated at the desk peered over her glasses at him, her unyielding gaze making him feel like an errant student in the principal's office. "May I help you, Dr. McCann?"

Now that he was here, his decision to look in on the patients seemed foolish, but he wasn't ready to be alone with his thoughts. "Yes, I'd like check on our, uh, guests."

"Most of them are sleeping and shouldn't be disturbed."

"Let me worry about their medical care, Miss…" He glanced at her name badge. "Montclair."

Her face flamed, and she looked contrite. "Of course, Doctor." She handed the clipboard that held the patient roster. "I'm sorry for my forwardness."

"No need. Your concern for the patients is admirable. I promise not to rouse them."

"Yes, sir." She returned her attention to the paperwork on her desk.

Ron strolled through the corridor, peeking into the dim rooms. He should apologize to the nurse. She was doing her job, perhaps better than him.

The new position was a mixed blessing. Exciting, challenging, and engrossing. Intricate and difficult cases that required a specialist came through almost daily, pushing his skills and abilities with each surgery. Filled with physicians at the top of their field, the hospital had a stellar reputation. The wounded who were treated here had higher percentages of recovery rates, and the number of amputations was a fraction of that at other facilities.

A glance into another darkened room. All was quiet with the exception of an occasional sigh. No moans, which meant the patients were resting comfortably.

He was making a difference. No. He was part of a team that was making a difference, but the group was incomplete. Doris wasn't on board.

What was she doing now? Had she landed on her feet? She'd disappeared without a trace, and the Red Cross refused to give him any contact information. Should he write his folks? He shook his head. That would open a can of worms that definitely needed to remain closed.

How would he find her? How would she react if he showed up? She'd made her feelings clear. He had to stop pining for her. He was a grown man, not a schoolboy. Surely, he could get over her given enough time.

His chest tightened, and he pressed his hand against his sternum. If he didn't know better he'd say he was having a heart attack, but he lacked any other symptoms. Angina? No. As a scientist, he could argue against the manifestation of physical pain associated with a breakup, but as a man whose heart ached from sunup to sundown since Doris walked out of his life, science couldn't stand up to reality.

He reached the end of the corridor, made a cursory peek into the room, and sighed. So much for his rounds being a diversion. Maybe someone had a card game going on in the dining hall. He could pretend to enjoy their company for a while, couldn't he?

Returning to the nurses' station, he handed Nurse Montclair the clipboard. "All is in order. Enjoy the rest of your evening."

Her smile didn't erase the wary look in her eyes. "You, too, sir."

With a wave, he left the building, then stopped at the curb. A light breeze smelling of flowers lifted his hair. Doris would know what was blooming this time of year, but did it matter now that she wasn't here to share the scent?

"McCann!"

Ron turned toward the strident voice.

Director Braverman hurried toward him, white jacket flapping like an egret's wings.

Waiting for the man to close the distance between them, Ron stuffed his hands in his pockets. Their interaction since the conversation that forced Doris away had been minimal. He submitted his reports and attended the periodic staff meetings during which he said little. Why would the man seek him out? He didn't seem angry, so that was a plus, but rumor said Braverman never worked past five o'clock. Fortunately, he'd only caught sight of Doris's accuser once from a distance. The lout must have known it was in his best interest to stay as far from Ron as possible.

Arriving at Ron's side winded and disheveled, Director Braverman smiled, his face set in an oily, disingenuous expression. "McCann. I have news."

"Couldn't this wait until morning, sir? I've been in surgery all day and most of the evening."

"You'll want this information." He crossed his arms and rocked back on his heels.

"Yes?" Would the man never spit out whatever he wanted to say?

"Lieutenant Halifax has been arrested. He was accused of attempted rape by one of the nurses, and the investigation turned up additional incidents of him getting, er, fresh with some of the women."

Ron narrowed his eyes. "When did this happen?"

"The investigation was conducted over the last three days, and he was picked up this afternoon. Miss Strealer is being contacted to take her statement."

"The statement you thought was false?"

"Careful, McCann. I'm your superior. I'll let your comment slide for the moment, but you may wish to show some gratitude. This means your girlfriend's reputation is saved."

"I wouldn't be so sure, Director."

———————◆———————

Doris gaped at her sister. "Last I heard you were back in the States. What gives?"

Emily rushed forward and enveloped her in a hug.

"You're scaring me, Em. Say something. Are Mom and Dad okay?" Doris pulled away. "The Red Cross wasn't supposed to say anything to anyone."

"Mom and Dad are fine. I've been in England for the last three months. The trip home was to get more training before my next assignment. I had two weeks of R and R, so I thought I'd look you up. Good thing I've got resources at my disposal. You're a tough one to find. What's going on, sis?"

"Where are you going to be stationed?"

"You know I can't tell you that, and stop trying to change the subject. I'm not going anywhere, so you may as well spill your story."

"I'm not ready to talk about things yet." Doris turned.

Lucy hovered nearby, her face impassive.

Doris slapped her forehead. "Lucy. I totally forgot you were here."

"That's obvious."

"I'm sorry. Lucy, this is my sister, Emily. She works for…well, actually I have no idea who she works for. I think she has to kill us if we find out. Emily, this is Lucy, one of my roommates, and a top-notch mechanic."

"Nice to meet you."

"A pleasure."

Lucy laid her wrench on the workbench. "I…uh…just remembered I have to go do something." She glanced at the clock on the wall. "I'll return in twenty minutes or so. Okay?"

Doris smiled. "Perfect. You're a peach."

"Yes, I am." She thwacked Doris on the shoulder with her rag, then stuffed it in her pocket before sauntering out the door.

"She seems nice."

"All of the gals have been good eggs. None of the usual drama or nonsense you get with a group of women. They're only interested in the job, and we don't have to worry about men thinking we can't do the work."

"Sorry things didn't work out at any of the garages at home. Dad told me that none of the men would hire you."

"Yeah, well, their loss. Sometimes, the rejection still stings, but I realized their attitudes are their problem. Don't know what will happen after the war as far as a job, but I take it one day at a time."

Emily squeezed her arm. "You're different. More self-assured but bruised." She studied Doris, forehead creased in a frown. "Talk to me."

"Fine, but you need to help me get this rig ready. The medic's on a deadline, and lives may be at stake." She handed Emily a flashlight and pointed. "Stand there and shine that thing wherever I'm working. Think you can do that?"

"You'd be surprised at what I know how to do now."

"I can't wait to find out, but I never had any doubts about you, sis. You had enough insecurities for the both of us. I hope that's changed."

"I was my own enemy at times." Emily nodded. "No one is going to be the same after this war, no matter how they serve. Especially all those women at home wondering where their husbands are or whether they'll return."

"Amen to that."

Doris leaned over the ambulance, renewed her work on the engine, took a deep breath, and for the second time in a two weeks, bared her soul to another woman about the chain of events that landed her in the MTC. Mrs. Wilkinson had listened without opinion or reproach; would Emily afford her the same respect?

Except for a periodic murmur that sounded like sympathy, Emily remained quiet. The tension in Doris's chest eased as the words tumbled from inside. Leaving nothing out, she included her convoluted feelings about Ron, and her dismay that she'd fallen hopelessly in love with him.

She tightened the bolt on the crankcase, then pulled her head out from under the hood, and took the flashlight from Emily. "Get in and turn her over."

"Turn her over?"

"Sorry. Start the car."

Emily slid behind the wheel, and seconds later the ambulance roared to life. Purring like a satisfied kitten, the engine ran smooth and sure.

Doris grinned and closed the hood with a bang. "Okay, cut it."

Her sister got out and brushed the dirt from her skirt. "You're a whiz, Dor. That medic's gonna be one happy guy."

"Thanks. I never get tired of tinkering on these babies." She sobered up. "As much as I love my job, I'm still miserable. How much longer before I get over Ron? Even Lucy's getting tired of me moping around. I try to hide my feelings, but she sees through me."

Emily drew her into a hug then kissed her cheek before letting her go. "Broken hearts take a while to heal, sis. But you're still hurting as badly as the day it happened. Maybe you're not going to get over him."

"Gee, that's uplifting advice." Doris blinked back the tears that sprang to her eyes. There was no way she could go from one day to the next with her heart in pieces. The pain was too great. "Got anything else, like get over it?"

"That's not what I meant. Maybe you need to give this guy another chance. Maybe your love is a forever kind of love and won't go away despite the world's best efforts to sabotage it."

Doris shook her head. "No. I can't go back to him. I already told him nothing could or would happen until after the war is over. If he still wants to pursue a relationship, we can talk about it then."

"Listen to yourself. Pursue a relationship? Talk about it? Love is not clinical. You can't hash it out in a debate or treat it like a contract. Honey, I see the way your face softens and how your voice caresses the words when you say his name. This kind of love can't wait until after the ceasefire." Laughing, Emily grabbed her arms. "Do I have to hogtie you and drive you there?"

"Ha, you don't know where he is."

"I uncovered you. I can easily find your doctor friend. Like I said, I've got skills you can't even imagine."

Heart pounding, Doris blew out a deep breath. Could she give Ron a second chance? Or was she already a distant memory for him?

Chapter Twenty-Eight

Ron's hands shook as he laid his folded shirts on top of his slacks inside the suitcase. Good thing he wasn't scheduled to perform surgery today. He hadn't been this nervous since the first operation he'd done during his residency. Memories washed over him of the beetle-browed supervising surgeon standing so close he could smell the man's breakfast on his breath. Afterward, the doctor told him that he had the best hands he'd seen in a decade, but that hadn't assuaged the jitters. Was the man still terrorizing residents, or had he finally retired?

He tossed his toiletry bag and some socks on top of his clothes. His gaze circulated the room then landed on his Bible lying on the nightstand. He picked up the leather-bound volume and stroked the cover. Can't forget this. No matter what happened with Doris, he'd be grateful for her walk of faith that led him back to his heavenly Father. Finally giving up control of his life, Ron had a fledgling peace that was growing as he learned to trust each day's outcome to God. The journey hadn't been easy, but the changes were worth the difficulties.

Two of the nurses had accepted Christ, and the crusty director regularly asked Ron questions about Jesus. Struggling to respond, the discussions forced him to dig deeper into the Bible so he could point the man in the right direction.

Thank You, God, for using me, a fallible man who makes mistakes. Thank You for Doris who helped me find my way back to the fold. Keep her safe, Father. Soften her heart toward me. My bumbling actions hurt her, so I'd appreciate the opportunity to make amends. And more.

In the distance, a clock chimed the hour, and he closed the suitcase lid with a bang. No more dawdling, McCann, or you'll miss the train. He glanced in the mirror and frowned. Lack of sleep over the past three days because of an influx of patients had rendered him haggard. His hair was shaggy, too, but time had not allowed for a trip to the barber. He rolled his eyes. Since when did he care about his appearance?

He grabbed his luggage and headed out of the room, slamming the door behind himself. He hurried toward the stairs then forced himself not to run down to the foyer.

"Have a nice trip, Dr. McCann." Sister Hatch, the head nurse, waved as she passed him on the steps. "You get that girl back, you hear?"

Apparently, nothing was a secret in the hospital community.

"I'll do my best." He grinned and held up his crossed fingers.

She pressed her palms together. "Prayer has a better chance than luck."

"Amen to that."

Whistling, he left the building and climbed into the waiting jeep. Would he return dejected or filled with joy?

Much to his surprise, the drive and subsequent train ride passed quickly, and he was soon in a bus on the final leg. Ron clutched the handle of his suitcase with slick palms. When a woman named Emily, claiming to be Doris's sister, contacted him with the news of Doris's whereabouts, he'd jumped at the chance to see her. Now that he was within minutes of their reunion, his stomach felt like a family of mice was roller-skating inside.

The trees outside the window waved at him, their edges tipped in red and orange. Still August, fall was arriving early this year. Colder temperatures wouldn't bode well for the troops. Frostbite and hypothermia cases increased during the winter months, but wounds didn't bleed as badly. A macabre choice for the boys in the infantry and armored divisions.

Bumping over the macadam, the bus swayed in rhythm to the tinny music rasping from the elderly driver's transistor radio. "Next stop, the MTC. All ashore who's going ashore." The octogenarian laughed at his own joke, his snaggletoothed grin lighting up his wrinkled face.

Brakes squealed as the bus rolled to a stop. The door popped open with a hiss.

Ron took a deep breath and stood. He ducked his head to prevent hitting the ceiling and squeezed between the seats to get into the aisle. He followed a trio of giggling girls in MTC uniforms off the bus. The door closed, and the vehicle chugged away.

"Excuse me, ladies." He raised his voice to be heard above the rumbling engine. "Can you help me find someone?"

They turned, and the blonde winked, a saucy smile on her face. "Sure, but why look any farther when you found the three of us?" Her companions laughed, and one of them eyed him like a steak on the grill.

He gave them what he hoped was a polite chuckle and shook his head. "Thank you, but…"

"Forget it, girls, this one's already in love." The pert blonde blew a large pink bubble then snapped her gum and shook her head. "Who ya looking for, honey?"

"Doris Strealer. She's a mechanic."

"We all are, honey. Hence the name: Mechanized Transport Corps." She gestured toward a stone building several hundred yards from the gate. "Chances are you'll find her hunched over some recalcitrant vehicle." She cocked her head. "Are you the reason she's been moping around like she lost her last dime?"

His face burned.

The girls guffawed, and the blonde elbowed the brunette on her left. "I think that's a yes. Well, Doris is a good egg, and you better be here to make things right." Her gaze turned flinty. "Don't let us find out you've hurt her again. Understand?"

"Yes, miss. I'm glad to know she has friends who watch out for her."

"You know what? We're going to escort you to her, see? How about that?"

His heart stuttered. Apologizing to Doris was going to be hard enough without an audience, but he couldn't blame the gals for protecting her. "Sounds like a dandy idea."

One of the brunettes grabbed his suitcase, and the other girls linked arms with him, marching him to the garage where his future waited.

Dust kicked up as they walked the dirt path. The sun warmed his back, and some sort of bird swooped and soared on the thermals overhead. A seemingly normal day, but the next few moments would change his life forever.

He stumbled on the threshold as he entered. A half-dozen vehicles were lined up in the center of the cavernous room, the smell of motor oil, grease, and gasoline clinging to the air. Tommy Dorsey warbled from the radio on a wooden table.

"Hey, Doris. Someone here to see you," the blonde called out then turned and glared at Ron. "Remember, we'll be watching."

One of the figures dressed in khaki-colored coveralls extricated herself from under the hood of an ambulance and turned. Hair tucked under a bandanna with a smudge on her chin and forehead, Doris looked at him, her mouth gaping. His heart hammered in his chest. If possible, she was even more beautiful than he'd remembered.

———————◆———————

Doris's swallowed against the lump in her throat. Her mouth was dry, her breath ragged. Ron was here. Standing in front of her, his expression a mixture of contrition, hope, and dare she think it, love. He was flanked by three of her colleagues, all looking smug. Too bad Emily wasn't here to gloat about his arrival, although she was probably the reason he was here.

She tucked at the collar of her coveralls, suddenly snug and confining. Aware of her rumpled appearance, she frowned. Why couldn't he show up at dinnertime, after she'd bathed and put on something flattering like a skirt and blouse? She yanked off the bandanna then raked her fingers through her hair. Her feet were rooted in place.

"Doris—"

"Ron—"

Hands outstretched, he walked toward her, his steps slow and unsure. "Doris. I've got news."

"You couldn't write a letter?" Her voice sounded harsh and unyielding, and she winced. What about giving him a second chance?

"I wanted to see you. Needed to see you." He stopped an arm's length away and dropped his hands. "Is there somewhere we can talk? He glanced over his shoulder at the trio who were still watching their interaction with wide-eyed, curious faces. "In private."

"We'll leave, but only on your say-so, Doris," the blonde said, her bubble gum popping.

Doris grinned, and the muscles in her back released their grip. Nice to know the girls were so protective. She nodded. "I'll be fine."

Disappointment colored their faces, but they pivoted and sauntered out of the building.

"Thanks. I'm glad you've got such good friends, Doris. People who take care of you."

"Yeah, this has been a good assignment. The work is challenging and interesting, and the others have accepted me. We're a close-knit group." She cocked her head. "What's the news you couldn't put in a letter?"

"Wouldn't you rather sit down?"

"Actually, the day is beautiful. How about if we go for a walk?"

"I'd like that." He clasped his hands behind his back as they made their way outside.

She stuffed her hands into the pockets of her coveralls and sighed. The sun glinted off the blond strands of Ron's hair and cast shadows on his angular features. He was as handsome as ever. He appeared to have lost some weight, but his shoulders were still square and broad.

He cleared his throat. "Lieutenant Halifax has been arrested on a charge of attempted rape. The investigation uncovered incidents of lewdness and....nevermind...no need to get specific."

Her stomach clenched, her lunch threatening to reappear. "How awful for her. She must be suffering terribly. I'll pray for her."

"Always thinking of others, aren't you? The director sends his apologies for his handling of your report, and he has stricken all references to inappropriate behavior on your part from your official record. In fact, he plans to submit a letter of commendation for your exemplary conduct under duress."

"Hoping to make up for his assumptions and pompous rejection of my claims, is he?" She shrugged. *Forgive me, Father. Help me be gracious.* "I'm sorry. I'm acting no better than he did."

"Understandable."

"Maybe, but Jesus would have me respond differently." She smiled. "Thanks for coming in person to tell me. I hate that so many others were subjected to the lieutenant's lasciviousness, but I'm glad he's been brought to justice. We should pray for him, too, although I admit that will be somewhat harder."

"Listen, Doris. There's another reason I wanted to see you. I've been miserable these past weeks. Every day was an eternity wondering where you were, what you were doing, and how you were holding up. I'm half a man without you. I bungled my proposal the last time. You were right to turn me down. I was trying to fix the situation. That's not a reason to get married."

"You've changed." She stopped and searched his face. "You're...I don't know how to explain it."

"At peace."

"Yes, that's it."

"All thanks to you. During one of the chaplain's sermons, I was convicted of my selfishness." He ducked his head. "And a host of other terrible traits. I didn't like the man I was and met with the padre to talk about it. I was already a believer, have been since I was a kid, but much like the prodigal son, I'd walked away from a real relationship with Jesus. Father White has helped me work my way back into a living, breathing bond with God."

"How did I do anything?"

"You never once seemed to waver in your faith. No matter how bad things got, you seemed to cling harder to God. I remembered that while Father White was preaching, and I wanted what you had."

"I'm happy for you, Ron." She crossed her arms to keep from throwing them around his neck and pressing him to her. He was a gorgeous man, but his integrity and newfound joy in the Lord were more attractive than any external appearance. Some woman would be lucky to have him. Too bad she'd let pride get in her way and run away. He was a good man to come and clear the air between them.

"Me, too." He reached for her hands. "But there's one more reason I'm here." He dropped to one knee.

She gasped and tried to pull away. Her heart stuttered.

He held his grip, eyes twinkling. "Doris Strealer, you are the most beautiful, inspiring, and good-hearted woman I've ever known. You challenge me to be a better person, to be a godly and upright man. You are on my mind when I wake up and when I go to sleep, and every moment in between. My life is a shell of what it could be without you. I love you. Will you make me the happiest man on earth and become my wife?"

Tears sprang to her eyes. She hadn't lost him. He loved her. He wanted to spend the rest of his days with her.

"Doris." His smile wavered. "Please say yes. I don't want to wait until after the war to see how we feel. I love you now and forever, and that won't change."

"Yes." Her voice broke. "I love you, too, and don't want to wait either."

He leapt to his feet and grabbed her in a bear hug, swinging her in circles as he laughed with abandon. A moment later, he set her down, a wide grin still on his face. "You've got your work cut out for you with this caveman."

She giggled. "I think God has already started the transformation."

"That He has." He bent his head and pressed his lips to hers, their warmth and invitation taking her breath away.

Her toes curled as tingles shot through her extremities, and she wrapped her arms around his neck drawing him closer. Their kiss deepened, and the sun burst from behind a cloud, heating her back. She pulled away and pointed to the gleaming ball of fire. "I think God approves."

"I know He does." He tucked her head under his chin, his arms enveloping her.

She snuggled closer and sighed. "How about a September wedding?"

THE END

What did you think of *The Mechanic and the MD?*

Thank you so much for purchasing *The Mechanic and the MD*. You could have selected any number of books to read, but you chose this book.

I hope it added encouragement and exhortation to your life. If so, it would be nice if you could share this book with your family and friends by posting to Facebook (www.facebook.com) and/or Twitter (www.twitter.com).

If you enjoyed this book and found some benefit in reading it, I'd appreciate it if you could take some time to post a review on Amazon, Goodreads, Kobo, GooglePlay, Apple Books, or other book review site of your choice. Your feedback and support will help me to improve my writing craft for future projects and make this book even better.

Thank you again for your purchase.

Blessings,

Linda Shenton Matchett

Acknowledgments

Although writing a book is a solitary task, it is not a solitary journey. There have been many who have helped and encouraged me along the way.

My parents, Richard and Jean Shenton, who presented me with my first writing tablet and encouraged me to capture my imagination with words. Thanks, Mom and Dad!

Scribes212 – my ACFW online critique group: Valerie Goree, Marcia Lahti, and the late Loretta Boyett (passed on to Glory, but never forgotten). Without your input, my writing would not be nearly as effective.

Eva Marie Everson – my mentor/instructor with Christian Writers' Guild. You took a timid, untrained student and turned her into a writer. Many thanks!

SincNE, and the folks who coordinate the Crimebake Writing Conference. I have attended many writing conferences, but without a doubt, Crimebake is one of the best. The workshops, seminars, panels, critiques, and every tiny aspect are well-executed, professional, and educational.

Paula Proofreader (https://paulaproofreader.wixsite.com/home): I'm so glad I found you! My work is cleaner because of your eagle eye. Any mistakes are completely mine.

Special thanks to Hank Phillippi Ryan, Halle Ephron, and Roberta Isleib for your encouragement and spot-on critiques of my work.

Thanks to my Book Brigade who provide information, encouragement, and support.

A heartfelt thank you to my brothers, Jack Shenton and Douglas Shenton, and my sister, Susan Shenton Greger for being enthusiastic cheerleaders during my writing journey. Your support means more than you'll know.

My husband, Wes, deserves special kudos for understanding my need to write. Thank you for creating my writing room – it's perfect, and I'm thankful for it every day. Thank you for your willingness to accept a house that's a bit cluttered, laundry that's not always done, and meals on the go. I love you.

And finally, to God be the glory. I thank Him for giving me the gift of writing and the inspiration to tell stories that shine the light on His goodness and mercy.

Read on for the first chapter in *The Widow and the War Correspondent*, book three in the "Sisters in Service" series.

New Hampshire, February 1944

Chapter One

Cora Strealer winced, gripping her pencil and notepad tighter as the burly man next to her trounced on her toes and cheered with the rest of the crowd. Whistles and applause filled the high school gymnasium, reverberating off the wood floor and cement walls. The largest room in her small town overflowed with members of the press, the public, and leaders of their tiny municipality anticipating the appearance of Rita Hayworth at the war bond rally. Someone had tried to purge the decades-old smell of sweaty teenage basketball players, but the acrid stink of perspiration clung to the crisp scent of bleach.

The last two rallies had been well-attended, but the announcement about the beautiful movie star's presence brought folks from miles around, including newspapermen from Boston who wouldn't normally give their event a second glance. She rolled her eyes. The only reason she'd gotten the assignment instead of Oscar Blanding, the other full time writer for their weekly paper, was his hospitalization. Much to his chagrin, he'd contracted appendicitis and required surgery to remove the offending organ. Bad for him, fantastic for her.

Would this be the big break she was waiting for?

She sighed. Probably not. As soon as he was released, Oscar would be back to writing the major news, and she'd be relegated to fluff pieces: graduations, engagement parties, retirement parties, and weddings with the occasional selectmen's meeting thrown in for good measure.

Her writing was good. Mr. Paxton, her editor, admitted that pearl several months ago during yet another argument as to why she wasn't allowed to cover feature stories. Maybe she could weasel her way into an interview with Miss Hayworth, then Mr. Paxton would have to let her do the article. Once it was published, the Associated Press or United Press could pick it up, sending it around the globe in one of the big newspapers. Then she'd get real press, a shot at the big leagues.

The jubilant woman knocked into her again, this time sending Doris crashing into the wall. She gritted her teeth and craned her neck to search for another spot from which to cover the event. Surely, there was a place she could stand and see everything without getting engulfed in the mass of humanity.

Sunlight glinted through the windows overhead. Doris squinted, and her gaze caught movement near the bleachers on the far side of the room. Perfect. Unless every other journalist in the room thought of hiding out underneath the wooden seating, she'd have a decent view without the chaos.

Fortunately, the benches weren't made of metal or the scrap collection committee would have snatched them along with the railings, cook pots, and other items that had disappeared over the course of the war.

She pressed her body against the wall and squeezed past the revelers. What would they be like when Miss Hayworth greeted them?

"Excuse me. Sorry. Coming through." Doris threaded her way along the perimeter of the room. She tried to ignore the frowns and glares from the attendees. Weren't they happy there was one less person in front of them?

Fifteen minutes of pushing and slithering brought her to the bleachers. She surveyed the undulating mass of people then ducked underneath the stands.

"Cora. I wondered when you'd come to your senses and join me." Her friend since elementary school, Amanda Norton stood under the bleachers, a mischievous grin on her face. Ebony hair swept up into a smooth chignon, and wearing a cobalt blue blouse with a black pencil skirt and stiletto heels, she looked every inch the executive she was.

"You look fabulous as always. Did you come straight from work?"

"Yeah, Dad said one of the family should represent us, and he had a bunch of phone calls to make."

"I still can't believe he gave you the manufacturing director's position over your brother." Cora pushed down tendrils of jealousy. What would it be like to have a challenging job and be taken seriously?

"Phil didn't want the job. He's happy tinkering in Research and Development." Amanda shrugged. "The board of directors was the difficult mountain to climb, but Dad convinced them I was the best person. I think they're waiting for me to fail." She shook her head. "Not going to happen. Anyway, enough about me. I don't wish the man ill, but Oscar's appendicitis worked out for you, huh?"

"I'm hoping to score an interview with Miss Hayworth, but there are so many big name reporters, I don't stand a chance."

Amanda smiled like a cat who'd finished a bowl of cream. "What if I were to tell you a certain movie star is going to tour our plant tomorrow, and I could get you time with her?"

Cora squealed. "You're the best. This might be my big break."

Cora threw back the covers and jumped out of bed. The wooden floor was warm on her bare feet as she hurried to the closet to select her outfit. The smell of pancakes filtered from the kitchen. Moving back home after her husband was killed with so many others during the attack at Pearl Harbor, she slept in the bedroom that had been hers since childhood. Her gaze went to the framed photograph of Brian. After two-and-a-half years, his death still seemed unreal. Trapped in the Arizona when the ship went down, his body hadn't been returned.

No body. No casket. No viewing. When would she stop looking for him to come through the door?

She closed her eyes for a long moment searching her heart. Sure, she missed Brian, but with their whirlwind courtship and even shorter marriage she hardly felt like a widow. Was she wrong to have those feelings? Her mother would be horrified.

Opening her eyes, Cora continued to run her hands over the clothes hanging in her closet. What did one wear when meeting a famous celebrity? Especially someone as elegant and refined as Miss Hayworth.

Her fingers fell on the sage-colored silk suit she'd worn for her wedding. Heart hammering, she pulled the outfit off its hanger and walked to the full-length mirror in the corner. She held the suit in front of her, studying her reflection in the glass. Blonde hair fell past her shoulders in a tangled mass, and her blue eyes picked up the green from the suit and seemed almost turquoise.

"Ugh. I look like a teenaged cheerleader with these freckles. No one would guess I'm thirty one years old." Rubbing her eyes that burned from lack of sleep, she yawned. How many times had she awakened with another idea for the interview? She glanced at the illegible scrawl on the top sheet of her notebook.

Time was wasting. She hurried to the bathroom and fifteen minutes later was dressed, ready to go. She stuffed the steno pad and extra pencils in her pocketbook and skipped down the stairs.

A car horn beeped outside, and she opened the door to wave at Amanda. Racing into the kitchen, she kissed her mother on the cheek and grabbed a piping hot pancake. Rolling it up, she blew on pastry before taking a bite. She snatched a napkin from the table. "Yummy as always, Mom. See you later."

"Have fun, honey."

"Thanks." Cora bit off another piece of the pancake as left the house and rushed to Amanda's car. Considered an essential war worker, she was assigned a C gasoline ration sticker, giving her more than the usual four gallons per week for most people.

Nearly out of her own rationed amount of fuel, Cora was thrilled when Amanda offered to pick her up. Bicycling to the plant in her suit hardly seemed like an option. She wiped her fingers on the napkin, then opened the door and climbed inside the backseat of the car. Her jaw dropped, and her breath quickened.

Seated beside her, Miss Hayworth smiled and held out her hand. "Mrs. Strealer? A pleasure to meet you."

Cora's heart threatened to jump from her chest, and she took a deep breath as she shook the movie star's hand. "Uh, actually I use my maiden name for my byline, but you can call me Cora."

"Perfect, and please call me Rita. We don't need formalities with just us girl here." She smoothed the skirt on her emerald-green dress then straightened the pillbox hat set on her gleaming titian-colored hair, orange highlights glinting in the early morning sun. Her smile was genuine as she patted Cora's knee. "How long have you been a newspaper woman?"

"Since high school. I got my degree in English then moved to Hawaii when my husband was assigned there. I wrote for the *Honolulu*

Star Advertiser, but after he was killed I moved back home, and now I write for the local paper."

"I'm sorry to hear about your husband."

Cora shrugged. "It was a long time ago."

From the driver's seat, Amanda gestured over her shoulder. "Cora's a great writer. I think she should apply to become a war correspondent. Especially with her experience at Pearl."

Face heating, Cora shook her head. "Amanda, Miss Hayworth…Rita…doesn't want to hear about my life."

"On the contrary." Rita smiled. "It will be nice to focus on someone other than myself. I appreciate what my celebrity status can do for the boys in the service and the country's morale, but being the center of attention is fatiguing. Tell me about the opportunity."

Licking her lips, Cora gulped. "In order to be a war correspondent overseas, I need to receive accreditation by the government which involves a lengthy background check and physical. Working for such a tiny newspaper, I'm not sure I'll pass."

"How about the Associated Press or United Press?" Rita cocked her head.

"Don't they have plenty of staff already?"

"This war spans the globe. There can never be too many reporters. I'll write you a letter of introduction to the London bureau chief for the UP. Will that help?"

Cora's eyes widened. "Well…uh—"

Amanda clapped her hands. "You're a peach, Rita. A recommendation from you should get our girl in."

"I'm happy to help. We gals need to stick together."

"Thank you, Miss—Rita, I appreciate the offer. I haven't decided to pursue going overseas."

"You can't let this pass you by, Cora. You're stagnating here in this one-horse town. Nothing is keeping you here. Certainly not this newspaper that doesn't appreciate your talent. I say you go for it. Don't you agree, Rita?"

Rita turned to Cora. "What do you want? Are you happy with your current position? You need to make the decision that's right for you, but I will say that if I hadn't made some changes in my life, I wouldn't be the star I am today. Sometimes shaking things up is good. Perhaps being a war correspondent will be the best thing to happen to you. Maybe not, but you won't know unless you try."

Cora slumped against the seat. "You're right. I'm stuck in a rut. Here in town, everyone feels sorry for me. They tiptoe around, afraid to talk about the war or my husband. A fresh start where no one knows about Brian might be just the ticket." Grinning, she straightened and crossed her arms. "Look out, world. Here I come."

Other Titles

Romance

Love's Harvest, Wartime Brides, Book 1

Love's Rescue, Wartime Brides, Book 2

Love's Belief, Wartime Brides, Book 3

Love's Allegiance, Wartime Brides, Book 4

Love Found in Sherwood Forest

A Love Not Forgotten

On the Rails

A Doctor in the House (The Hope of Christmas Collection)

Spies & Sweethearts, Sisters in Service, Book 1

The Mechanic & the MD, Sisters in Service, Book 2

The Widow & the War Correspondent, Sisters in Service, Book 3

(June, 2020)

Mystery

Under Fire, Ruth Brown Mystery Series, Book 1

Under Ground, Ruth Brown Mystery Series, Book 2

Under Cover, Ruth Brown Mystery Series, Book 3

Murder of Convenience, Women of Courage, Book 1

Non-Fiction

WWII Word Find, Volume 1

Linda Shenton Matchett writes about ordinary people who did extraordinary things in days gone by. She is a volunteer docent and archivist at the Wright Museum of WWII and a trustee for her local public library. Born in Baltimore, Maryland, a stone's throw from Fort McHenry, she has lived in historical places most of her life. Now located in central New Hampshire, Linda's favorite activities include exploring historic sites and immersing herself in the imaginary worlds created by other authors.

Website/blog: http://www.LindaShentonMatchett.com

Facebook: http://www.facebook.com/LindaShentonMatchettAuthor

Pinterest: http://www.pinterest.com/lindasmatchett

Amazon: https://www.amazon.com/Linda-Shenton-Matchett/e/B01DNB54S0

Goodreads: http://www.goodreads.com/author_linda_matchett

Bookbub: http://www.bookbub.com/authors/linda-shenton-matchett

CPSIA information can be obtained
at www.ICGtesting.com
Printed in the USA
LVHW042137010520
654880LV00005B/1223

9 781734 708523